STEP YA GAME UP PUBLISHING
EVEN FICTION NEEDS TO BE BELIEVABLE!

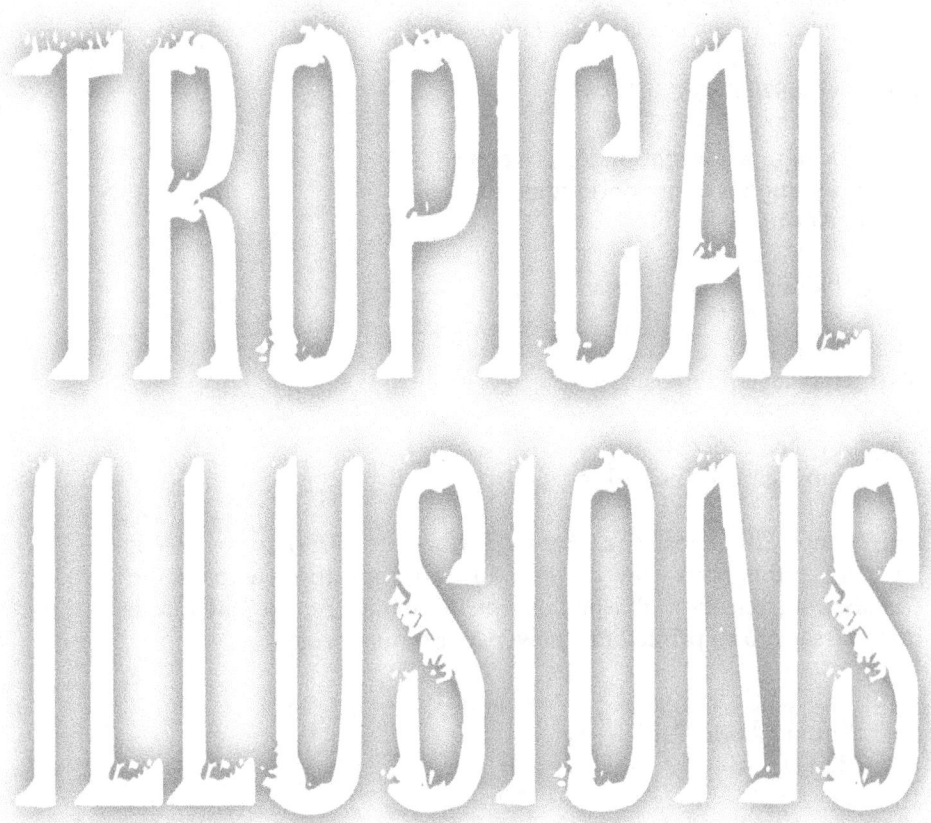

TROPICAL ILLUSIONS

A NOVEL BY

JOHN BOWENS

ISBN: (13) 978-0-9853303-0-9

Cover design: www.mariondesigns.com
Inside layout: www.mariondesigns.com
Editor: Andrea Baker

Tropical Illusions/John Bowens

Step Ya Game Up Publishing
P.O. Box 25706
Charlotte, NC 28227
www.stepyagameuppublishing.com

First Printing April 2012
Printed in U.S.A.
10   9   8   7   6   5   4   3   2   1

DEDICATION

Frances "Mama2" Howard

And, in memory of:

Luisa "Luki" Henry

PROLOGUE

"Yes!" I was thinking as the steaming hot water rushed from the shower head and covered my body, *"I'm the man! I'm the mutha fuckin' man!"*

I soaped up twice making sure I hit the major areas with an extra scrub, and then I just stood under the water and enjoyed the warmth and comfort which was the 'after party' of yet another conquest.

Stepping out of the shower, I grabbed a burgundy towel and began to dry off. I couldn't resist an impulse to wipe steam from the mirror over the sink just so I could steal a glance at the handsome reflection staring back at me with that knowing look. I had to smile!

"Yes!" I felt like a mutha fuckin Don!

'Good things come to those who wait!' That's what they say.

I wrapped a few squares of toilet paper around my hand and gave the mirror an official wipe down. Water was glistening on my bald head, my golden brown complexion had a radiant look to it, and my grey eyes sparkled.

"If loving you is all that I gotta do— I don't wanna do anything else!" I was singing out loud. Damn! Good pussy got the kid thinking he can sing!

I let the towel fall to the floor and began flexing my biceps and triceps in front of the mirror. I stuck my chest out in an authoritative gesture, silently admiring my physique. I thought about Tasia in the next room waiting for me patiently. She was probably still lying in bed. I still found it hard to believe that baby girl finally gave me some rhythm, after months of playing cat and mouse. It was no wonder Tasia was playing hard to get, baby girl was drop dead gorgeous! She had to be one of the most beautiful women I had ever seen. Her jet black hair fell to the small part of her back, her brown eyes were slanted as if she was of Asian descent. and her skin was creamy like coffee with sugar and a splash of milk. To top it off, she had some full pink lips that could only be described as luscious, her breast were the size of Honey melons, just the way I like 'em, and her firm ass was enough to have the Pastor of any church praising the Lord. And Tasia's breath smelled like strawberries . . . even in the morning, after just waking up, her mouth tasted like fresh fruit. The sex was illmatic! I mean, I didn't think it was possible for baby girl's shit to stink. I almost lost my cool when she licked me all over, but instead I regained my composure and returned the favor. When I entered her, she sucked in air as if she hadn't been breathing for the past twenty-five years of her life. She grabbed me hard and pulled me to her as if she wanted us to be one, or as if I wasn't penetrating deep enough for her satisfaction. Sounds of a wounded animal escaped from her, and that's when I knew I was doing my thing! I knew I was satisfying her—she was crying! I kissed her tears, and gently placed her legs over my shoulders. I had my hands positioned on the bed as if I was about to do some wide push-ups, and I was stroking! I felt like the boss of all bosses sitting on top of the world with the prettiest of all women literally crying for my love.

If I only knew why she was crying! If I only knew.....My ego would've been crushed! Maybe I would've had a chance to pull back . . . but I couldn't have known! It was impossible for me to know.

So there I was, looking in the bathroom mirror, confident as if I knew the mysteries of life.

I put on the beige terry cloth robe, compliment of the Holiday Inn, took one last glance in the mirror and then made my way back into the room.

I froze! It felt like I just walked into the twilight zone. I couldn't believe what my eyes were seeing! Tasia was sitting at the edge of the bed with my nine millimeter jammed into her mouth! This didn't make sense!

When Tasia saw me come out of the bathroom, she used her thumb to cock back the hammer and closed her eyes real tight. My mind was racing!
"Tasia, No!!!!!" I yelled.

I dashed toward the bed and heard an empty click as the hammer fell down on an empty chamber. I was so glad that I had enough sense not to leave a bullet in the head. I dove on top of Tasia grabbing the gun from out of her mouth and fighting to get possession of it. She was crying and fighting me desperately, pleading with me to let her die. To say that I was confused would be an understatement! I finally got possession of the gun and pinned Tasia to the bed. I looked at her in bewilderment. She was sobbing uncontrollably and I wondered what in the hell was going on. I felt violated, hurt, and confused! Here I was, exuberant over the fact that me and shorty had finally hooked up, and I expected her to feel the same.

I kept Tasia pinned to the bed until she calmed down, and then I pulled her to me putting my arms around her protectively as I whispered words of encouragement into her ear. She told me that she was sorry, over and over again. I wanted to know *why*. Why would someone so smart and beautiful want to take their own life?

My momma always told me to be careful what you ask for because you just might get it; thus, I didn't have to wonder any longer. Tasia poured her heart out to me! She told me of the tragic dilemma that pushed her to the point of self destruction. It was un-*fucking* believable! I blanked out........I flipped!!!

In order for you to fully understand what happened next, you would have to hear the whole story. Then and only then could you begin to understand. Then and only then could you even *think* about judging me.

Until then, fuck all of ya'll! Fuck the Police, fuck the media, and mutha fuck all of my so called friends who didn't wait to hear my side of the story. Matter of fact, fuck you too if you read this story and still can't feel my pain . . . .

Only God Can Judge Me!!!

SIX MONTHS AGO . . .

CHAPTER 1

For some reason, he felt compelled to lie. There was no way he was about to tell Tasia that he was going to strip club. She would never understand. So instead, he offered a typical explanation: "Boo, I'm going out with the fellas for a little while . . . do you need me to pick anything up on the way in?"

They were in the kitchen. Tasia rinsed off the plate she'd been washing and set it in the rack to dry with the rest of the dishes from dinner. She gave Jeff a confused look as she dried her hands on a towel.

"No . . . I don't need anything, *but*, I would like to know where you're going at ten 'O clock at night."

Jeff didn't appreciate being questioned as if he was a child, but Tasia had a gangsta girl way of talking that turned him on.

He was leaning against the refrigerator with a fitted Yankee cap pulled low over his face.

Tasia was standing in front of him looking edible, wearing nothing but a t-shirt and panties, and that alone almost tempted him to change his plans.

He reached out and pulled Shorty to him, his hands caressing the back of her lower thighs and sliding up until he was palming her firm round ass.

"You know Antwan is home from Afghanistan, but he's only gonna be here for a week. Me and Chip was thinking about taking him to get a few drinks and that's about it."

There! That wasn't even a lie. They *was* going out for drinks, Jeff just conveniently left out the part about the drinks being served in a strip club.

Tasia laid her head on his shoulder and gently ran her fingers across the little mole on his neck. She knew she had a solid relationship with Jeff, and she trusted him because he never gave her a reason not to. Never the less, she still felt a sense of insecurity on the rare occasions that her man, for one reason or another, left the house at odd times of the night.

"Just be careful, you hear me? And don't be out there giving what's mine to no hoochie mommas!" She said playfully as she reached down to massage the quickly growing bulge she felt pressing against her.

"At least I know a part of you doesn't want to leave," she added.

"Yeah, well, don't start nothing you can't finish . . ." Jeff advised and then continued: "The way I be putting it down on you, I wouldn't have the energy to give another chick the business! Besides, I love you too much to even think about messing up what we have."

Before things got too heavy and Tasia could respond to his challenge, they were interrupted by the sound of a car horn blowing persistently.

Jeff made his way to the front window and saw Antwan's black 540 BMW sitting outside with it's nineteen inch chrome rims spinning. Jeff almost felt guilty, but his mind rationalized - *'I'm only going to a strip club, it's not like I'm cheating.'*

He gave Tasia a big hug and kiss, and he was out the door.

If he could've predicted what was about to transpire, Jeffery Wilson would've kept his ass home, like his heart was telling him to.

Once Jeff made his way into the back seat of the BMW, Chip gave Antwan the directions to Gordon's, a well known strip club on Hillside Avenue in Queens, New York. He thought about directing him to 'Dreams' on Jamaica Avenue, but, there was a stripper at Gordon's name Tropical that was absolutely phat to death.

"Tasia let that ass out the house, huh?!?" Chip yelled, even though the music wasn't loud.

"Imagine that!" Jeff responded.

Chip was the big mouth of the three, and it was normal for little slick shit to come flying out his mouth.

"It ain't my fault you can't maintain a relationship for more than ninety days," Jeff said putting him in his place, and then continued; "But fuck all that sucker shit, what's up with the international baller here???" Jeff asked smacking Antwan on the back of the head.

"Stop playing.... you sucka for love ass nigga!" Twan said catching a glance at Jeff through the rear view mirror, and smiling.

"Oh, you believe everything Chip tell you, right? I bet he didn't tell you about that nasty little chicken head that let him lick it, but he didn't get to stick it!"

"Get the fuck outta here!" Antwan said excitedly, feeding into the drama.

"That's a mother-fucking lie! You lying and your breath stink." Chip yelled.

"Oh, you didn't tell me—"

"--Yeah, I told you that, but that was suppose to be between me and you. You's a petty ass nigga, Jeff! A mother-fucker can't tell you nothing." Chip said turning around in his seat and looking as if he was really offended.

"That's why I miss ya'll crazy asses!" Twan said.

They laughed and joked about the old days and did some catching up on the present during the ride to the club. When Twan finally parked the car across the street from Gordon's, Jeff had his first premonition. This big mouth idiot Chip had a gun! It wasn't nothing big, it looked like a .380, but it was a gun nonetheless; and guns meant trouble.

"What the fuck you need that for?" Jeff whined.

"What, this????" Chip yelled trying to stuff the gun down in his boot, "This ain't nothing but a little insurance."

"Insurance? Insurance for what, Chip? We just came to have a few drinks with Twan....."

"Man, listen....." Chip started as he got out of the car: "If you gonna cry, what the babies gonna do? I told you it ain't nothing but a little insurance. If niggaz don't act like niggers, then I won't have to bust a cap in a nigger ass. Now I don't know about y'all, but I'm going to see some tits and ass!"

Chip started to cross the street and was walking toward the club. Jeff felt like beating the shit out of him but Twan calmed him down.

"Don't even trip, Jeff . . . sometimes we have to think for other people so let it ride. Let's just go up in there and have a good time like we planned."

As soon as Jeff left the house, Tasia took a long hot shower, flossed, brushed her teeth, and grabbed the remote control before getting into her bed. Her feet were cold and she wished Jeff was there to keep them warm.

It was 10:45pm, so she decided to catch the last fifteen minutes of Comic View, and she hoped she would be able to stay up until Jeff came home.

Little did Tasia know, but, tonight was the night that would alter the direction of her life forever. She couldn't have known the events that were taking place that would affect her so deeply..... but tonight was just the beginning, and Tasia was in the dark.

"Face down, ass up— that's the way we like to . . ."

Chip was screaming along with the song and obviously having a ball! Antwan and Jeff seemed to be enjoying themselves also, but Jeff continuously had to ask himself why he even dealt with Chip. They were friends since elementary school, but, besides basketball, Jeff was beginning to realize they had nothing in common.

A dark skin dime piece with thickness in all the right places was poppin' that thang on the small stage. Chip was sticking dollars in her G-string and trying to put his fingers in her pussy at the same time.

"Yeah baby!" Chip yelled when she politely guided his

hands to her perky breast before quickly moving away from him.

Jeff felt that dude was too obnoxious, but, instead of letting Chip ruin his night, he decided to get drunk. Pissy drunk! He waved at the pretty little barmaid in the black cat suit and ordered a double Hennessey and a beer to chase it down.

From their seats by the stage, Jeff observed a small group of thugs entering the club.
These guys were wearing platinum around their necks, diamonds in their ears, and they had an air of confidence about themselves as if they owned the place.

They made their way to a few empty seats by the stage, and shortly after, a barmaid was setting two ice buckets with bottles of Cristal in front of them.

They sat through about two more songs before Tropical came out and put the whole joint in a frenzy!

Jeff tried not to get too excited over the strippers, but Tropical just about blew his mind!

She was wearing a purple wig and some purple shorts that couldn't contain her entire ass. Baby girl had an ass like Buffy, and her whole persona was captivating. She had juicy, full, suck-*able* lips, shining with lip gloss, and she walked on the stage as if she was the baddest bitch in the building.

Jeff found himself waving a ten dollar bill at her. Tropical walked over giving Jeff crazy eye contact, she glanced at the bill he was holding unimpressed and shook her head from side to side.

Jeff was in a trance! Tropical turned around giving him a banging back shot and seductively peeled her shorts off. Her legs were locked back and Jeff almost bust off in his pants! Tropical glanced back to see if she had his undivided attention, knowing full well she did.

She was wearing a purple thong that looked like it was glowing in the dark, and when she turned around she slyly pulled it to the side exposing a neatly trimmed bush and an ear ring in the perfect spot.

Jeff quickly made the ten dollar bill disappear and his hand resurfaced with a crisp fifty. He tried to put it in the purple scarf tied around Tropical's thigh, but she backed out of reach and smiled at him before proceeding to work the stage. She allowed everyone to spend money except for Jeff, leaving him baffled.

Chip was going crazy, being loud, and punching Twan on the arm.

"I told you, kid! I told you! Look at Jeff ...... that sucka for love ass nigga is stuck! Girlfriend is the truth— I told you!"

Chip guzzled down a shot of Henny, and when Tropical's segment was over he motioned for the barmaid.

When she came over, Chip asked her how much would it cost for a private show with Tropical. The barmaid went to look into the matter and came back quickly... but she directed her words toward Jeff.

"It seems like Tropical is interested in somebody herself. If you're interested, you and your friends have been invited downstairs for V.I.P. treatment."

Jeff desperately wanted to fight his desires, but the alcohol he consumed made it useless. He gave the barmaid a twenty dollar tip, and they all were instructed to follow her.

Jeff was a little tipsy, and unfortunately, he accidentally bumped into one of the thugs he scoped out earlier, causing the guy to spill his drink.

Before Jeff could say excuse me, the guy had turned around and furiously pushed him off balance.

"You need to watch where the fuck you're going!" He yelled, staring at Jeff threateningly.

"My bad, partner." Jeff said controlling his anger.

"You fuckin' right it's your bad, and I'm not your partner, chump!" The guy shot back.

"Man, listen" Chip yelled, and then continued, "He said it's his bad . . . You need to sit ya ass down and be easy— you're missing a good show!"

The thug tried to swing at Chip, but one of his boys held him back. The Bouncers alerted to the trouble made their way to the scene.

"I wish your faggot ass would!" Chip yelled.

"Come on Chip, let it go." Antwan pleaded.

"Nah man, I'll bust a cap in his ass— he don't know me!"

Jeff and Antwan pulled Chip away and they proceeded to follow the barmaid down a flight of stairs that was located right next to the bar. She led them to a small room that was dimly lit and had couches against almost every wall, and she instructed them to get comfortable until Tropical and some of the other girls arrived.

50 cent's 'In Da Club' was banging through the speakers when the five exotic dancers entered the room. They were already in a zone, and they worked the small room as if they were still on stage. Tropical made her way over to Jeff and was dancing seductively.

The dark skin dime piece that Antwan was in love with was

doing the Beyonce' dance and her ass was jiggling like it didn't want to stop! Shorty called herself V.I.P.!

When Antwan had the chance to ask why she called herself V.I.P. she responded, "Because this ass is *exclusive!*"

Shakey had some big ass titties, and she was bouncing around the room living up to her name. The other two dancers were out of control! These chicks were bi-sexual and they wanted the world to know about it! Chip wasn't concerned with the world, all he knew was that they definitely had his attention. They were dancing together and touching on each other as if they were the only ones in the room.

Chip couldn't control himself, he got up off of the couch he'd been sitting on and joined them. Shawna and Shateva didn't seem to mind at all. They put Chip in the middle and began taking his clothes off. Chip thought he died and went to heaven!

"Go Shorty— it's your birthday! We're gonna party like it's your birthday!" He was singing and palming ass at the same time.

Twan was standing up getting a wall dance from V.I.P., she was bending over touching her toes and backing that ass up against his crotch.

Shakey was dancing in the mirror, watching as she touched herself sensually and sucking on her huge mouth watering torpedoes.

It was going down real big! By the time the D.J. upstairs took it to the dirty south and had the Ying Yang Twins hollering, "*Shake it like a salt shaker*" Chip and his new lesbian friends were ass naked lying on the floor getting it in!

Shawna had the dick in her mouth sucking it like a bomb pop. Chip was putting his licky-licky game down on Shateva's pretty little pussy, and Shateva had her face buried between

Shawna's legs.

While all this was jumping off, Tropical was in her own little world seducing Jeff. She couldn't believe how much Jeff resembled Corey. Corey was her boyfriend that was killed in a motorcycle accident over a year ago, but her heart still cried out for him.

When Corey got killed, Tropical freaked out! She started doing things that she would have never done had Corey still been alive. Becoming a stripper was one of those things, but, the bills needed to be paid and her daughter had to eat.

Corey had been to Tropical what the blanket was to Lynus on Charlie Brown. He was her security; her rock. So when she saw Jeff sitting by the stage looking just like her Boo, her pussy was instantly wet. She knew she wanted to be intimate with him and it had nothing to do with money.

Now she was giving Jeff a lap dance, and her pussy was throbbing! She had her hands underneath Jeff's shirt caressing his body and she was leaning over playing with her tongue in his ear.

Jeff's dick was harder than a fifty pound bag of frozen neck bones!

Tropical reached down and unbuttoned his jeans, quickly pulling down his zipper and freeing the long brown snake. Pre-cum was dripping out of the head and she slid her knees to the floor and began sucking the juice off his helmet. Jeff wanted to bust off right in her mouth, but Tropical was digging in between the cushions of the couch and came up with a condom. Jeff managed to hold off.

Tropical used her teeth and opened up the package holding the condom. She ran her hand up and down the dick a few times and then expertly sucked the condom onto his hardness. In one motion she was up, pulling her thong to the side and mounting Jeff. Jeff was in total submission. He put his hands on Tropical's hips and enjoyed the ride. Tropical used her pussy muscles and clung to the dick. In her zone she was fucking Corey. She bent over and stuck her tongue in his mouth.

Jeff couldn't stand the rain! Any guilt he may have felt was temporarily forgotten as he bust a huge nut and got caught in the rapture.

"Ooooooo Weeeee!" He sung, breathing heavily.

Everything was all good until Tropical climbed her fat, round ass from off of him. Jeff felt like the ultimate sucker for love. The guilt returned like a boomer rang, and to top it off, he looked down only to see his bare, deflating dick staring back at him.

'Damn, damn, damn!!!' He thought, thinking of Florida Evans from the seventies sitcom 'Good times'. It was a funny thought, but Jeff wasn't laughing.

The one time he allowed his desires to get the best of him, and the mother fucking condom broke.

CHAPTER 2

Baby boy sported the bulletproof baseball cap tilted to the side as if he was making a fashion statement as opposed to protecting his dome. His bulletproof vest protruded under his camouflage fatigue jacket, making his small frame appear stocky.

Shakim maneuvered his black Range Rover through the streets of Jamaica, Queens, New York City as if he was on a battlefield.

The word was out, Shakim was sitting on six digits, and that alone was enough to leave the haters envious. To make matters worse, Shakim moved out of the 'hood,' and the streets was talking.... they was saying that son wasn't keeping it real!

One jealous dude went as far as shooting at the jeep while it was parked across the street from Baisley Projects, on Foch Boulevard; between Guy R. Brewer and Long Street.

Shakim heard through the grapevine that it was Gabe from building one in Baisley, and, he also got word that Gabe and the boy Steve-O was studying his moves.

These thoughts invaded Shakim's mind like U.S. troops in Iraq!

Shakim use to hustle in Baisley! He use to get money with the little homie Buttons before the incident that left one of the Carmichael brothers paralyzed, and Buttons was sentenced to 12 and a half to 25 years in prison for attempted murder.

After that, Shakim chilled the fuck out until his Uncle Raheem came home from the Feds and put him up on the Real Estate game. Ever since then he blew up like the U.S.S. Cole and never looked back.

He still had friends in Baisley that he kept in touch with, mostly females, but for the most part son escaped from the hood.

That explained the bulletproof attire and the Tec. 9 submachine gun resting in his lap. Jay-Z's Reasonable Doubt CD was in the disc player and Shakim amped himself up as "Can't Knock The Hustle" blared from the speakers of his jeep.

Quiet is kept...Sha was thinking with his other head. Common sense should've told him that he was no longer welcomed in the 'hood,' but no, he couldn't find the discipline to stay away from the rendezvous that he regularly used when he wanted to see Black Nicole.

As he drove down 116th Avenue, his libido went into third gear just from thinking about shorty! Black Nicole was a stallion!

Shorty had an ass like Jessica Rabbit, her oral game was on one million, and all Shakim had to do was buy her a pair of fifty-four elevens (Reeboks) and her black ass was happy. Shakim smiled and fondled the growing bulge in his pants as he turned into the parking lot behind building five in Baisley. It was after eleven p.m., but not quite eleven thirty, which was the time he told Nicole to meet him.

He parked in a space that afforded him a view of building five's back exit, and he immediately killed his head lights. After scoping the vicinity for Nicole or any signs of danger, Shakim impatiently dictated to the car phone to dial Nicole's number. The sound system automatically lowered it's volume, and Nicole answered the phone on the first ring.

"Hello?"

"Blackie, what da fuck are you doing?" Shakim said as if he was annoyed, "You up there smoking crack? If you think I'm gonna be sitting out here all night you on something!"

"Ooh, I'm sorry Sha, I thought you said eleven thirty. You're downstairs?"

"Boo listen, I'm about to leave! I been out here for damn near a half an hour—"

"Wait! Don't leave me, I'm coming right now, O'kay? Don't go nowhere!"

"Blackie... Why you still on the phone?!?" Sha asked and hung up before she could respond. He reclined his seat and gripped the Tec.9 that rested in his lap.

While Shakim waited he checked his phone and saw that he had five text messages. Two of the messages were from Renee, his ex-girlfriend, she claimed to have something very important to talk to him about. One message was from Ki-Ki, she was like his baby sister, she just-wanted to remind him that he was suppose to stop by to pick up the Stop Snitching DVD. Then there was a message from Sean Howard, the real estate broker, who more than likely had some news on the latest property they were checking out. And the final message was from his uncle Raheem.

Shakim voice activated his cell phone and called Raheem immediately. The phone was answered on the third ring.

"Unc, holla atcha boy!"

"Son, what do you have a phone for? I called you about

two hours ago." Raheem was on some smooth shit for real, he spoke nonchalantly.

"Come on Fam, I see what time you called me, you called at 10:30. I was in the middle of something important, that's why I'm just calling back."

"Something important huh . . . You spoke to Sean?"

Nicole came out of the back exit of building five walking fast. *Damn, shorty ass is so fat you can see it from the front* Sha thought as he lusted for shorty.

She came and glided into the passenger seat smiling like she knew what he was thinking.

"Sha???" That was Raheem on the other end of the phone.

"Yo!"

"What you doing???"

"Listening to you!"

"'What I say?"

"Err . . . say it again."

"You's a funny nigga! I asked you did you speak to Sean?"

"Oh, nah, I was gonna call him after I spoke to you."

Sha looked in the rear view mirror and backed the Range out of the parking lot.

"If you're gonna follow your dick around let me know now so I can let you do you. If it was up to you we'd probably be living in card board boxes. Call Sean and then get back at me."

Click!

"That's that bullshit!" Shakim said before calling Sean Howard.

"What's up sexy?" He said looking at Nicole giving a

16

little squeeze to her thigh.

She didn't respond, she was just smiling and licking her lips like there wasn't nothing to talk about.

Sean Howard answered on the first ring, Sha put him on the speaker.

"Sean, it's Sha, what's up?"

"Good evening. I tried to call you about an hour ago, did you get my text?"

"Yeah, I was in the middle of something, what's up?"

"Okay, this is in reference to the property on Hillside Avenue that you inquired about. I spoke to my connect and the price quoted on that specific property is six hundred and seventy- five grand. My connect says that the lady will let it go for six hundred and fifty. The building has six, three bedroom apartments, the condition is fair.....My advice is that we don't pay more than six hundred grand."

"At six hundred even what's the down payment gonna look like?" Sha was trying to sound like a seasoned business man. He knew the numbers he was throwing around had Nicole ready to suck his dick just because.

"An educated guess would be ten percent, that'll be sixty grand not including closing costs."

"Did the lady take out a second mortgage loan on the joint?"

"No, and I know where you're going with that. The truth is I'm two steps ahead of you. I already set up a meeting with Skip over at Chase Manhattan to see if he'll approve the loan, and I mentioned it to Ms. Brown— that's the lady's name who's handling the property. She may go for it, but it's going to cost us."

"Alright, get the paperwork together on that and I'll be over in the morning to take a look at it. I'm gonna call my uncle right now and let him know what's what."

"What time in the morning, Sha, because I'm meeting with Skip at 9:30?"

"How about eleven?"

"Eleven is fine."

"Alright cool, I'll see you then."

"Alright then, have a good night."

By the time Sha got off the phone with Sean Howard, he was two minutes away from the Marriott, so he decided to wait until he was in his room before calling Raheem back.

Shakim owned a condominium in New Jersey that was right across the George Washington bridge, about a twenty minute ride, but, he wasn't stupid enough to let just anybody know where he lived. So, most of his sexual escapades were carried out in hotels, and every once in a while he would utilize the back seat of his jeep.

"You hungry?" Sha asked when they were finally in the hotel making their way through the quiet corridor to the suite he reserved.

"Uh un, you?" Nicole lost the permanent grin and now wore a calculating expression. Sha knew shorty was out of her league, and he took full advantage. He wondered... when would women realize that a man, an official dude, would never buy a cow if he could get the milk for free.

"Yeah, I'm hungry, but the kid ain't thinking about food."

Once they crossed the threshold and entered the room it was on! Sha grabbed shorty and pinned her against the wall, palming her ass aggressively and throwing tongue in her mouth.

He tossed the bulletproof baseball cap across the room, put the Tec 9 on the floor and began to undress.

Nicole was reaching for the mandingo, tugging on it and helping Sha get out of his clothes.

"Take your clothes off!" Sha said impatiently.

"Wait!"" Nicole said, dropping to her knees and taking the entire dick in her mouth. Sha was beginning to think that shorty enjoyed giving head even more than he liked receiving it. And that was cool with him!

Shorty was sucking his balls and playing with the dick all over her face, and that shit felt good as hell.

Nicole's facial expression was a bonus enhancement. Sha grabbed his rock hard dick and began smacking Nicole softly with it in her face while she opened her mouth and let her tongue hang like the real bitches did.

At that point, he remembered that he had to call his uncle back. The bomb ass head that Nicole was giving up was almost enough to make him say fuck it, but not quite.

Unc made sure a nigga was eating, so Sha wasn't volunteering to fuck that up.

"Go get in the shower, I'll be in there in a minute - I have to call my uncle back real quick."

"Call him later!"

"I can't, now go 'head before I get mad."

Nicole got off her knees and took her clothes off. Sha watched her with a hard dick in his hand until she went in the bathroom and he heard the water come on. He was about to go call Raheem, but he had to piss badder than a mother fucker.

He went in the bathroom and lifted up the toilet seat. Nicole popped her head out of the shower curtain.

"Mind your business, Blackie."

Nicole sucked her teeth and closed the curtain.

"You are my business, and stop calling me Blackie!"

Shakim was about to respond but was cut off by a fierce pain in his penis. It felt as if someone were sticking needles into the head of his dick! He immediately stopped the flow of urine, sucking in air and letting out a small cry.

Nicole's head popped back out the shower curtain.

"What's wrong???"

"Nothing! I caught a cramp - mind your business!"

Nicole sucked her teeth again and disappeared behind the curtain.

Shakim held his breath and tried to piss real quick. It turned out to be the longest piss of his life, at least it felt like it. Baby boy had to literally relieve himself in spurts. He couldn't believe his luck and all he could think was, *not again.* Shakim was burning!

CHAPTER 3

The alarm on the clock radio went off at 5:30a.m., saving Tasia from a restless night.

With a heavy hand she reached over and turned the alarm clock off. Tasia couldn't believe that Jeff had stayed out all night. She threw the covers off of her and got out of bed, immediately picking up the phone and calling Jeff only to reach his voicemail.

Tasia was dying to hear his excuse. What could he possibly say? *Boo, I was drunk and crashed out at Chips crib.* He better not come at me with no lame shit like that!

Tasia was pissed! She put on a pot of coffee and made her way to the bathroom. After using the bathroom and brushing her teeth she decided to call Jeff again. *'This mother fucker had better been in an accident or something!'*

No sooner than the thought crossed her mind, Tasia began to panic!

'Oh my God! Jeff may have been in an accident!!! I'm sitting here thinking all negative and my boo may be hurt, or worse. .... No! I shouldn't think like that.'

Tasia picked up the phone and began calling all of the local hospitals. Still not finding her love, she reluctantly called the city morgue. She was relieved that Jeff wasn't there either, but Tasia was still worried nonetheless.

She drank an extra strong cup of coffee and proceeded to prepare herself for work. Donning an attractive, yet conservative skirt set, Tasia checked her appearance in the mirror. Satisfied that she was presentable, she made sure the stove was off, checked her pocketbook to make sure she had everything she needed, and she was out the door.

It was a beautiful day outside on this third day of September. The sun was up, shining brightly, but the truth was that the summer was drawing to an end. Labor Day weekend was just two days away - two days! The birds was singing and Mrs. Peterson was raking leaves in her front yard. Everything appeared the way it was suppose to be, except for one thing....... Tasia couldn't find her best friend.

"Hi Mrs. Peterson!' Tasia said in the most cheerful voice she could muster.

"And good morning to you too, child!" Mrs. Peterson responded without looking up from her task.

Tasia made her way to the red Honda Accord sitting in her driveway parked in front of Jeff s black Ford Explorer. After deactivating the alarm, she got inside the Accord and started it's engine. As she let the car warm up for a minute, Jeff s Ford Explorer caught her attention through the rear view mirror.

"Jeffery Wilson, you better be o'kay, and if you are, you have a whole lot of explaining to do!" Tasia said aloud. She put the car in drive and drove to work.

Tasia found a parking space a block away from her job on Hillside Avenue. She grabbed her pocketbook from the passenger seat and was out of the car, activating the alarm and making sure the doors were locked.

She began walking toward the offices of Colossal Realty and mentally preparing for another day at work when a voice stopped her.

"Excuse me, miss.....you dropped something."

Tasia stopped abruptly, looking down, scanning the ground around and behind her for the possible item or items that may have fallen. Finding nothing on the ground she quickly set her sights on the culprit who had cried wolf. He wore a friendly smile.

"If you went for that, I know you'll go for this - can I talk to you for a minute."

Tasia looked the man up and down like, *No this nigga didn't!* Granted, he was cute. and he definitely knew how to dress, but this was absolutely the wrong morning for the bullshit.

"Yeah, that was slick, but as you can see I'm really not amused." Tasia said with a spicy attitude.

"Sweetheart, I wasn't really trying to be funny, I just wanted to get your attention. And I admit, my method may have been a bit childish." The man said as he closed the distance between them.

They were in front of the used car lot that was on the next block from Tasia's job. People were walking by, rushing here and there, and Tasia impatiently yet courteously waited for the man to continue.

"I just wanted to tell you that you have an amazing air of confidence about yourself, and, I think it's sexy as hell." He finally said.

He watched Tasia closely, hoping his words generated a positive response, but he was in for a rude awakening.

"Thank you! Are you finished?" Tasia asked, not

bothering to hide the sarcasm.

"Well, actually I'm not." The man shot back, appearing to be amused by the subtle challenge, and then continued: "My name is James Carter, I own this car dealership!"

The man was certain that this revelation would impress Tasia and change her whole demeanor, but again, he was in for a rude awakening.

"And???" Tasia asked, visibly upset. She didn't appreciate the tacit implication that she should be moved by the fact that the man owned his own business. That was some chicken-head shit, and as far as Tasia was concerned, a person's worth couldn't be determined by their material gains. *Whatever happened to character? Integrity? Go figure!* Obviously, James Carter was on a totally different page.

"And, If you ever consider buying a car......drop by and I'll see if I can't pull a few strings. We can make a decent trade for your Honda, for a beautiful woman such as yourself, I'll make it my business to see that you only drive Beamers and Benzes! As a matter of fact, let's discuss this over breakfast - my treat, I know the perfect place."

"No thank you! I'm perfectly happy with my Honda, and as for us having breakfast— I'm already spoken for. Have a nice day!"

And Tasia was gone.

When they walked out of the club, the cool breeze immediately helped to clear Jeff's brain just enough for him to be alerted to the danger lurking nearby. The thugs they had the confrontation with earlier in the club were about fifty feet away standing next to a black Cadillac Escalade. The guy who had pushed Jeff was laying in the cut, and as soon as he spotted them exiting the club he instantly began walking in their direction. Jeff, sensing trouble, instructed Antwan to go get the car.

"I think we got some unfinished business!" The guy said, approaching with his hands in his pockets.

Jeff started to explain that it was just a misunderstanding that they had, but it was too late! Instantaneously, everything went coo-coo for cocoa puffs!

With murder in his eyes, Chip raised his hand clutching the black .380 and the gun discharged twice, it's bark disturbing an otherwise silent night.

"Bhop! Bhop!"

Jeff was horrified! Simultaneously, he was powerless over what was transpiring. It seemed to be happening in slow motion. The thug began falling backwards from the two shots to his head from close range . . . he was dead before he even hit the ground.

"Blakka! Blakka! Blakka!"

The thugs from the black Escalade began returning fire! One of their bullets found its mark, hitting Chip in the shoulder and spinning him around, causing him to fling the .380. The gun slid under a parked car and Chip turned around and ran like the cops were chasing him.

"Blakka! Blakka!"

"Buc! Buc! Buc! Buc! Buc!"

Jeff dove to the ground and crawled in between two cars. Shots were ringing off like crazy, and bullets could be heard smashing into metal and whizzing pass.

"Where the other one go?" A paranoid voice yelled.

"He's over there son, he's behind one of those cars!" Someone yelled back.

Jeff was scared to death! The thugs were closing in on him trying to kill him, Antwan was nowhere to be found, and to top it off, Jeff caught a strong urge to take a mean shit.

"Blakka! Blakka! Blakka!"

The bullets were tearing into one of the cars that Jeff was between. *'Where the fuck is Antwan with the car?'* He thought as he crouched lower to the ground. *'This nigga Chip ran, and... Oh shit, the gun,'* Jeff began scanning the ground as if his life depended on it, at the same time he was praying, and as fate would have it, his prayer was answered. *Thank you God!* Chip's .380 was under one of the cars!

After being bombarded by another fusillade, Jeff moved like a worm until he could reach out and grab the .380. The thugs were getting closer, and Jeff came face to face with a tragic dilemma-- kill, or be killed!

"There that nigga go right there son!"

"Bhop! Bhop! Bhop!"

Jeff made the decision to try to stay alive! That was the good news! The bad news was that Jeff had just wasted the last three bullets in the gun. *'Damn!'*

Fortunately, those three slugs were just enough to slow the thugs down and buy Jeff some much needed time.

"Come on!" Jeff yelled. Being the excellent poker player that he was, he decided to implement his bluff game. "We can do this all night!" He continued with more confidence than he actually felt. That's about the time he heard, "Whoop, Woop!" and flashing lights could be seen speeding in their direction

26

from a distance. Jeff heard car doors slamming and tires as they screeched on the pavement! He looked up just in time to see the black Escalade tearing ass around the corner.

Jeff made his move! He dipped low on the sidewalk and began running in the opposite direction. He only needed to make it to the corner and he would be home free. His heart was beating a hundred miles an hour, and if nothing else, the boy Jeff was happy just to be alive. Never the less, just as he was approaching the corner a blue and white patrol car appeared out of nowhere. The officers jumped from the vehicle with weapons drawn!

"FREEZE!" One of the officers yelled. Jeff froze in his tracks.

"DROP THE WEAPON, NOW!!!" Another officer yelled.
'Oh shit!

Jeff didn't even realize he was still clutching the gun! Ever so slowly, leaving one hand suspended in the air, he laid the .380 on the ground, all the while he was anticipating the sound of gunfire and bracing himself for the impact of the slugs that would more than likely invade his body. All praise was due to God they never came, but Jeff knew he was fortunate.... the NYPD was notorious for busting their guns, yet the powers that be had spared him. For that he was thankful, but there would actually come a time during this ordeal when Jeffery Wilson would wish that he was dead. Less than a hundred feet away a man was just killed......and Jeff got caught with the smoking gun.

CHAPTER 4

Dr Abraham's office was located on Rockaway Boulevard in the heart of the ghetto. This was the place that the hood depended on to deal with (S.T.D.s) Sexually Transmitted Diseases. It was 8:30 in the morning and Raheem and Shakim were in the small lounge waiting for the doctor to call Shakim's name.

What Raheem didn't know was, Shakim had a rough night. Baby boy refused to drink anything because he was afraid that he would have to urinate again, and to make matters worse, he had to use every ounce of strength he had just to keep his hands off of Nicole. That was a challenge!

Without a doubt, Shakim's number one weakness was women - baby boy was insatiable! So much so that he truly didn't have a clue to help him figure out which of his female companions had cursed him with a venereal disease. He did narrow it down though.... it had to be either Shelly or Tamika because those were the only ones he was intimate with within the past seven days besides Stephanie. Stephanie was a good girl, so he eliminated her as a suspect. Shakim had been creeping with Stephanie for over two years and he trusted her, but she was too damn gullible and naive' for him to ever consider her as his main girl.

A short and chubby white lady wearing a nurse's uniform peeked in the waiting room and told Shakim that Dr. Abraham was ready to see him.

"That's you, dirty dick!" Raheem said, looking up from the book he was reading. Raheem was being facetious. He shook his head as he watched his nephew follow the nurse through the door that would lead him to one of the various examination rooms.

'Hopefully a shot in the ass and a few doses of penicillin will solve Shakim 's problem' Raheem thought before getting back to his book. He was reading, 'Real Estate Finance and Investment Manual' by Jack Cummings.

Raheem was a serious dude! He was the backbone of a crew of drug boys that was prospering in the crack game in the late eighties. Dude was still spending money from eighty-eight for real! His sister Beverly (Shakim's mother) use to bag up drugs and count money for him until she messed up and started getting high. Beverly fell victim to crack cocaine and it was just a matter of time before she became an official base head. Raheem blamed himself for turning her on to the game, but he still cut Beverly off completely when he found out that she was bartering sexual favors for drugs and money to support her habit.

It wasn't long after that when the Drug Enforcement Agency came through in U-Haul trucks and helicopters and hauled Raheem and his crew off to the Metropolitan Correction Center (MCC) in lower Manhattan.

Ultimately, Raheem was sentenced to 12 years in prison, but, truth be told, his incarceration was a blessing in disguise. Raheem took full advantage of his time by attending Newport Business Institute and earned a Bachelor of Arts Degree in Business Management. He began eating healthy foods, exercising religiously, and reading voraciously. In particular, he enjoyed books such as 'Eyes to My Soul' by Tyrone Powers, 'Seven Habits of Highly Effective People' by Stephen Covey, and one of his favorite books was 'How to Make Big Money in Real Estate' by Tyler Hicks.

It was in Lewisburg Penitentiary where Raheem made the transition from street hustler to Sunni Muslim. He was always inclined to do what was right so it was a natural transformation. Raheem learned how to read and write Arabic, enabling him to study the Qur'an and ponder upon it's meaning in it's original language. In time, he found himself humbled, and in awe of the creator, and he began to be thankful for even the smallest of things.

After serving close to ten years in prison, Raheem returned to society a changed man. He was mentally, physically, and spiritually on top of his game. He possessed detailed yet flexible plans to obtain financial success, and a part of his plan was to give back to the community that he once helped to destroy.

In approximately one year after his release from prison, Raheem was back on his feet. Diligent research of banks offering real estate loans uncovered a number of foreclosure properties.

With strong desires of being prosperous, Raheem made trips to federal government offices such as HUD (The Department of Housing and Urban Development), the IRS (Internal Revenue Service), and the FHA (The Federal Housing Administration), and obtained a quick College education on foreclosures. The free information he received from these organizations proved to be priceless.

Raheem visited foreclosure properties on weekends and

sometimes he found time to do so after work on weekdays. He kept a little pocket size notebook in which he noted the condition that each property was in. Granted, these appraisals were conducted with an amateur's eye but, Raheem was confident that he knew the difference between a good and bad property.

Next, Raheem taught himself bidding techniques. He did this by examining each Property in his notebook and placing an asterisk next to the ones that appealed to him. He also wrote down the price that he would offer on each of the properties. Raheem knew that you had to bid on foreclosures offered at government sales because their rules require public open bidding. With this knowledge, he attended auctions and mentally pretended to bid on each of the properties in his notebook. He then observed what price each property actually sold for and he compared that price with the one he predicted. Raheem practiced this technique until he felt comfortable enough to finally get his feet wet. In the beginning, he lost quite a few bids because he was reluctant to go out of his predetermined price range. However, Raheem learned that patience is truly a virtue one morning when he finally hit pay dirt......he bought a duplex from a government agency for $31,000. A fellow bidder whom Raheem had seen around was consulting his own notes, and he advised Raheem to sell the duplex as opposed to keeping it and trying to fix it up. It turned out to be a badly abused property, but, with the man's help, the duplex still sold 10 days later for $45,000---- giving Raheem a fourteen grand profit.

This is how Raheem met and befriended Sean Howard. Sean Howard was a shrewd real estate broker, and he and Raheem developed a strong rapport seemingly overnight. Sean recognized a passion in Raheem that seemed to be absent in so many of Raheem's counterparts. This was a man whom, despite his background, refused to be held back, and Sean Howard recognized that a good relationship would without doubt be beneficial to the both of them. He became the boost that Raheem needed to take things to the next level.

Still, Raheem never forgot where he came from, and he adhered to his plans of giving back to the community.

His first real challenge was to help his nephew. Shakim was a hardheaded dude, but Raheem vowed to be patient with him. After all, Raheem felt he was partly to blame for Shakim's mother, Beverly, being lost to the streets.

With the help of Sean Howard, Raheem helped Shakim purchase an apartment building for $500,000. A mortgage lender agreed to lend eighty percent of the appraised value on the property which in this case was four hundred grand. So all Shakim had to do to take over this income property was to come up with a hundred grand for the down payment. Raheem had planned to take care of that for his nephew but, to Shakim's dismay, at the last minute, Raheem said that he wouldn't be able to do it because his money was tied up in other deals. So Raheem called the seller and said:

"Listen. I have to pull out of this deal, because I can't afford to pay $500,000 with the hundred grand down payment for this property."

The seller was shocked because she was determined to sell the property so she could move to Atlanta.

"Well, what price would make you go through with this deal???" She asked, trying not to sound desperate.

Raheem smiled...........Sean Howard was right again! "I could buy it for three hundred and fifty thousand." He told the lady.

"What about three seventy-five?" She asked.

"You know what? You drive a hard bargain, but you got yourself a deal— I'll take it!" Raheem replied as if he was doing the lady a favor.

With a $400,000 loan already approved, the deal went through. Shakim inherited his first property and Raheem walked away with twenty-five grand in his pocket. That was a sweet deal.

Raheem put his book down just as Shakim was coming from out of the examination room. He was hoping that Shakim was done because the smell of rubbing alcohol blended with disinfectant was starting to give him a headache.

Shakim was walking with a limp.

"What's wrong with your leg?" Raheem asked, getting up and stretching.

"Man, true story.....the doctor shot me in my ass with a big ass needle. That shit got my right leg feeling numb"

"Oh yeah? That's crazy! You ready to go?"

"Uh huh! Give me a minute, I gotta get this medication."

Raheem walked outside while Shakim went to fill his prescription.

It was a beautiful day and Raheem was happy just to be alive.

Still, he felt an urgency to convey to his nephew that life was not a joke. When Raheem was in the game, a shot in the ass was common, but, those days were over.

The Human Immunodeficiency Virus (HIV) and Acquired Immune Deficiency Syndrome (AIDS) now had the world under siege. What would normally result to a shot in the ass, now resulted to long hospital stays, habitual medication consumption, and ultimately an occasion to wear black.

It was actually depressing for those who took time out to ponder. At a time when HIV and AIDS had the world with her back against a wall, people were more promiscuous than ever before. Women were proud to be seen in public half naked, no longer leaving anything to the imagination. Men were following their lower desires and manufacturing a million reasons why they refuse to use condoms. And the media was exploiting sex to the highest degree! It was so bad that a man couldn't even watch a toothpaste commercial without his dick getting hard off of the beautiful half naked women that was used to help promote the product.

Raheem opened the door of the Range Rover and slid into the passenger seat when he saw Shakim limping out of the clinic. It was almost ten a.m. so they had more than an hour to kill before meeting with Sean Howard.

When Shakim got inside the truck, Raheem instructed him to drive to the International House of Pancakes on Hillside Avenue.

"You hear me, Unc" Shakim began before letting out a loud belch, "When I find out which one of those nasty whores burned me, I'm gonna break my foot off in somebody's ass!"

They were just finishing up their breakfast at IHOP, still picking over their food and shooting the breeze. The place was almost packed to capacity and the atmosphere exuded the smell of blueberry pancakes, fried eggs, and crisp turkey bacon. There was a buzz in the restaurant as the forty to fifty patrons were enthralled by individual conversations.

"Say excuse me! And next time cover your mouth." Raheem responded, dipping a slice of buttered toast into the yoke of his sunny side up eggs before devouring it.

"And what I tell you about referring to women as whores and bitches?"

"My bad, excuse me! I'm just mad as hell, and you'd be too it they stuck a metal q-tip in the head of your dick---- Aaaaargh!!!" Shakim squirmed in his seat just thinking about it.

"Well.........Did you ever consider using a condom?"

Shakim began doing a little dance, singing Ole Dirty Bastard— *Ooh baby I like it raw!*

People at nearby tables, not knowing the content of the conversation, giggled at Shakim's little performance.

Raheem just shook his head. He wanted to laugh because his nephew was a crazy dude, I mean hilarious, but this was a life or death issue, and Raheem didn't want Shakim taking it lightly.

"I'm just messing witcha, Unc ....." Shakim said noticing the disappointed look on Raheem's face, then continued, "But true story, I don't feel nothing when I wear a condom. No disrespect, but I like the way pussy feel!"

"Well you need to lay down in the dirt and get use to that feeling, because that's exactly where you're going to be if you don't start taking life more serious. Listen to me nephew... I did things that the devil would be ashamed of, so in no way am I trying to be holier than thou, but, for real- for real? You need to find a good girl and settle down. It's either that or start choking the chicken. If not, I'm going to mess around and lose you....... and this is one time, nephew, this is one time that I beg Allah not to be able to tell you— I told you so!"

On that note, a little cute waitress with a beautiful phat ass came to find out if they wanted anything else. True to form, Shakim responded.

"Nah, we straight . . . but you can write your name and telephone number down on a piece of paper, and nine times out of ten, I'll probably holla atchu later on tonight."

Shorty got on her job immediately! She was trying to get one of their attention from the minute they stepped foot out of the Range and came up in the spot.

Raheem just shook his head in defeat. Sometimes he felt as if he would come out better talking to a wall.

Nevertheless, the time was now 10:45a.m., and they had pressing business with Sean Howard. So Raheem allowed the sucka shit to blow Pass him, and focused his mind on bigger and better things.

CHAPTER 5

Jeff was in the bullpen stressed out! The detectives over at the 103rd precinct had refused to give him a phone call unless he signed a written confession, and that wasn't about to happen.

A few of the diabolical officers had roughed him up a bit but, they really didn't care if he signed the damned confession or not because the fact of the matter was that Jeff had been caught with the smoking gun. For that reason alone, the boys in blue were celebrating.

Jeff sat on the hard wooden bench with a brown paper towel, trying to remove the black ink from his fingers. After being fingerprinted, asked a thousand questions, and the arresting officer completed his paperwork, Jeff was transported to Central Bookings on Queens Boulevard. There he was fingerprinted again, and photographed, before being placed in a large cell with ten to fifteen other prisoners who were just coming through the system.

They were fed powdered eggs on a hard roll, and coffee that tasted like dirt, and the living conditions were uncivilized. Besides the underarm funk and foul odor coming from men whom haven't bathed in days, the toilet which was in a corner of the cell fully exposed reeked of urine and defecation! To make matters worse, someone clogged the toilet up with too much toilet paper so it wouldn't flush, and if you pressed the issue the toilet threatened to overflow.

Jeff went from bullpen to bullpen finding tantamount if not similar conditions before he finally arrived in the dungeon; a small crowded cell right next to the courtroom. A lawyer from the Legal Aid Society who resembled Urkel came to advise him about the arraignment proceedings, and he basically informed Jeff that there wasn't much to be done except enter a plea of not guilty, and hope the judge set a bail.

Unfortunately, the judge had denied bail, and now Jeff was in the bullpen stressed out.

The sound of wooden boxes, filled with leg irons and handcuffs, being dragged across the floor sent a message to the prisoners in the nearby holding cells . . . a bus was preparing to leave for Riker's Island!

A spectrum of emotions shrouded the holding cell that Jeff was in as the Correction Officer began calling out names.

"Thompson?"

"Right here!"

A young African American man stepped forward, a grim look on his face as he reluctantly submitted to being shackled like a slave being transported to an unfamiliar land.

"First name?"

"Troy!"

"Date of birth?"

"5/26/71"

"See the Officer by the door!"

One by one, the predominantly African American and Hispanic clientele was questioned and handcuffed, and then systematically bound together by leg shackles.

As Jeff waited to be called, he studied his surroundings. The frustration on the faces of his counterparts was evident, but, by far, fear was the dominant emotion.

"Wilson???"

"Yo!!!"

"Pay attention! First name?"

"Jeffery!"

"Date of birth?"

"March lst, 1975!"

"Step forward!"

The Officer put the cold steel bracelets around Jeff's wrist and then shackled his leg to that of a fat guy's from Far Rockaway that every one took to calling Big Man. Big Man was rocking a black Sean John jean suit that was dirty from laying on the floor. Like Jeff, this was Big Man's first trip to Riker's Island, and he was trying not to show it but he was scared to death! Everyone had heard the horror stories about Riker's Island, and now a bus load of minorities was on their way to this formidable place.

"This is it." Big Man said, trying to synchronize as they made their way to the back of the line.

"You won't be smiling on Riker's Island!" someone up front said aloud.

"I know one thing, they better feed my black ass! I don't care where we go after that, I'm hungry" This was an old head whom had just cuffed up. He was the last man so he had the benefit of being chained up by himself.

A C.O. used a huge metal key and unlocked a gate and the prisoners slowly filed out and shuffled toward the bus.

"You'll be fed when you get where you're going." a

black officer said assuredly.

"Where we going, C.O.?" someone asked, full of concern.

The officer smiled, happy to be able to answer the young man's question.

"C-74"

"Handcuffed on back of a bus, forty of us . . . "

Dude from Forty projects came through the system so often it was almost like a second home. He was spitting lyrics from C.R.E.A.M. on Wu Tang Clan's 36 Chambers CD, and amping himself up with the dexterity of a hardened criminal.

"Life as a shorty shouldn't be so rough!"

The blue and orange Department of Corrections bus was hauling ass down the Grand Central Expressway en route to Riker's Island.

Jeff was mentally preparing himself for the unexpected. He couldn't really concentrate because this bird ass nigga was singing out loud and the scary dude sitting next to him was beefing for rap. Jeff wasn't a disrespectful person but, he honestly wanted to tell Big Man in the seat next to him to shut the fuck up!

Big Man weighed in at about 250 pounds, yet for the entire bus ride all his scared ass talked about was how everybody had to stick together.

As the C.O. driving the bus seemingly concentrated on hitting every pothole on the highway at high speed, Jeff watched the scenery pass by as if he was in a bad dream. They passed

Flushing Meadow park, Shea Stadium; home of the New York Mets, La Guardia Airport, and then finally the long, formidable bridge that delivered them to their new home--A.K.A. The Island!

After the Officers in charge dropped off their weapons, they proceeded to C-74.

Jeff hardly had time to evaluate the sudden and unexpected turn his life was taking. He was a man accused of murder, being thrown into a snake pit, and his first priority inevitably became survival.

Jeff was lonely, confused, and afraid, not to mention tired. He wanted to cry, but to do so would be looked upon as weakness, and by no means was he volunteering to display that. So he tapped into the rich treasure chest of strength that his ancestors had employed to survive over four hundred years of brutal slavery. Jeff put his head up high and bravely confronted his immediate reality. He stayed in sync with Big Man, taking small measured steps as they walked into what many people would describe as hell on earth.

"Welcome to the Terror dome!" someone was screaming in an agonizing tone.

A bus load of new jacks had entered the building and the sharks smelled blood in the water.

"Welcome to the Terror dome!!!"

Most of the guys in the group were petrified! Big Man thought he could literally feel the hair on the back of his neck standing up.

Dude from Forty projects appeared to be in love with the electrical energy flowing through the air.

"Yeah, yeah, yeah! Woo, woo, woo!!!" he hollered at no one in particular.

A guy in one of the holding cells recognizing the display of bravado immediately began an interrogation.

"Yeah, yeah, woo, woo! Ayo money, where ya'll coming from?" he yelled as if he was speaking for the benefit of everyone in the bull pens.

"Queens House!" dude from Forty responded.

The place went into pandemonium as the bullpens in unison began degrading and belittling the entire borough of Queens. While Jeff and his group were being uncuffed, the hecklers were repeating the name Queens in feminine and soft voices.

"You didn't hear a peep from a place called Queens!" the spokesman cried out.

Jeff and most of the group ignored the comments and proceeded to be processed. Some guys literally kept their gaze to the ground.

Dude from Forty laughed and spoke out loud as if he was unmoved by the disrespect.

"These niggas can't possibly know who da fuck I be!" he said with a cool confidence.

"Who you, Money? Who you be?" somebody yelled.

"I be dat nigga Rondu! The nigga who had the whole mod.8 on smash damn near the whole last year!"

Mod.8 was short for modular 8, and it was one of the housing units in C-74. Still, the prisoners in the bullpens were tougher than the audience at amateur night at the Apollo, and they weren't impressed.

"Never heard of you!" someone yelled.

"Who you???" came another heckler.

One of the Officers who appeared to be paying the ruckus no mind, smiled and questioned the guy who seemed to have the biggest mouth.

"Warren, what housing unit are you on?"

"I'm from Four main, the house of pain!" the guy responded with pride.

"Oh yeah?" the Officer asked and then continued, "So you're over there with Big Freeze from Rockaway Boulevard, right?"

"Nah, Big Freeze is in Four Upper!"

"Oh, that's right.., them boys from Queens got Four Upper on lock. Williams, you remember Freeze don't you?"

Rondu looked at the CO. with a smirk. Officer Edey was from Jamaica, Queens, and she was making it known to everyone within listening distance that Queens was definitely in the building.

"That's my Mutha fucking man!" Rondu stated as a matter of fact.

"Warren, I think you need to ask Freeze about Rondu Williams when you get back to the block." Officer Edey said.

The guy stood there with the jackass look but, he tried to clean the situation up so he wouldn't look like a cold sucker.

"If he's Freeze' people then he cool, what you say your name was, Rondu.?"

"That's what the fuck I said!"

"You need something to smoke?"

"You mutha fuckin right I need something to smoke, I

need some matches too!"

By the time Jeff and his counterparts finished being processed and made it to modular six; the New Jack dormitory, it was almost ten o'clock at night. The phones would be turned off at eleven.

Rondu commandeered one of the two phones and held it hostage until 10:50pm, and then showed some love by allowing Jeff to hold down the last ten minutes.

Jeff was relieved! He had sacrificed a much needed shower in hope that he would be able to make a phone call. He hadn't spoken to Tasia in almost two days and she had to be worried sick by now. He wiped the phone off with his shirt, took a deep breath, and dialed his number.

Tasia picked up on the first ring and Jeff wanted to cry when he heard her say: "Jeff???"

CHAPTER 6

Even though Steve was notorious for bustin' his gun, by consensus he was a funny ass dude. Steve was the type of person who would do practically anything for a good laugh.

One time he was in McDonalds during rush hour with a few cats from his crew. Steve squeezed out a loud fart and then shouted in a funny voice: "Oops! Look what you made me do!"

Granted, some people would argue that there was no humor to be found in a grown man imprudently passing gas, but, those had to be the people who didn't know Steve.

Without a doubt, Steve was about his business! He was a well paid enforcer for Kaymel, a minor drug dealer with a major team. But for those who knew Steve as a friend, it was easy to see that he was a good dude.

This was exemplified one day when Steve was at Marty's Barbershop on Jamaica Avenue and 161st Street; right across the street from Jamaica Savings Bank. Steve was waiting for his little man Gabe to finish getting his hair cut, and not being one to sit still for more than five minutes, Steve decided to wait outside so he could get some fresh air. When he walked outside, he noticed a dirty, stinking bum laying on the ground by the barbershop talking to himself.

"Hey! You talking to me, old head?" Steve asked the

man, knowing good and well he wasn't.

The bum was in his own little world and he wasn't paying Steve any mind.

Steve's crazy ass walked over and kicked the bum on the bottom of his dirty ass combat boots with just enough force to gain his attention.

"What the hell are you over here talking about, Old head? Put me down on what's going on." Steve said as if he was genuinely interested in what the bum had to say.

The far away look that was in the bum's eyes quickly dissipated as he came out of his zone and focused in on Steve. In a humble and sincere tone, he asked: "Man, why you messing with me? I aint bothering nobody."

Steve was amused, but, at the same time he felt kind of ashamed for disturbing the man and breaking his peace. So, he humbled himself and offered the vagrant an explanation.

"I'm not messing with you, Old head, I was just trying to be friendly. Are you hungry? I apologize if I offended you, but come on, let me buy you something to eat, a hot dog or something."

The Old head was irresolute, he truly didn't know how to respond. He was actually skeptical of anyone crazy enough to talk to him, let alone show him compassion, because he didn't believe that he deserved it. He was a nasty, stinking bum, and a loser in his own eyes, with no friends or family. As far as he was concerned he earned the right to wallow in his own misery.

The only thing was that, Steve, with all of his shortcomings, for some reason or another felt compelled to do a good deed. He held his hand out to help the bum to his feet. Old head hesitated, his cynical nature rearing it's head, but then he reluctantly accepted the helping hand. Steve helped dust the man off and then they made their way into the Texas Weeners restaurant right next to the barbershop.

As soon as they entered the establishment, an old cowboy looking guy behind the counter began to get excited.

"Hey you! Remove yourself from this restaurant! I told you once I'll tell you a thousand times-- no bums allowed! Please leave before I call the cops."

The cowboy clearly didn't share Steve's compassionate sentiments, and Steve couldn't help but to wonder how the man would feel if one day he found himself in a similar position.

The bum, however, froze in his tracks and looked as if he was preparing to retreat. Steve peeped the move and quickly spoke up.

"He aint going nowhere, he's with me, And I think you need to treat your customers with a little more respect."

"Come on guy, you can't be serious!" the cowboy complained as if he was the one looking for sympathy, "This bum is stinking up the whole joint!"

'Yeah okay,' Steve thought before busting off a loud fart. Brrrrrnt!

"Good God! If you think he stink, wait until you get a whiff of that joint right there . . . now, let me get three chili dogs and a Hawaiian punch. Old head what you want?" Steve asked as he theatrically fanned his ass.

The bum squinted his eyes at the giant menu that hung over the grill behind the counter. The old cowboy surrendered to the situation and just hoped he could get the bum out of there before the rush hour crowd came in at lunch time.

That was how Steve got down, he was an enforcer by

trade but a good dude by nature.

Now as Steve parked his Dodge Charger in front of Kaymels beauty parlor, he had his game face on. Kaymel was standing out front with two of his lieutenants, Doonie and Blast, speaking intently. Other members of the crew were in proximity on point, no one was laughing or joking and there was hardly anyone engaged in conversation.

Steve concluded that something had happened... something serious. As he exited his charger, Steve noticed that Green eyes was missing.

'Where the fuck is this nigga at' Steve wondered. Green eyes was Kaymel's second in command and it was rare for one to be seen without the other.

As Steve approached Kaymel, his fear was confirmed, something vital had taken place. Kaymel, who was normally in control of his emotions, was standing there with tears in his eyes, and Doonie and Blast looked as if they had lost their best friend.

Steve looked deep into Kaymel's eyes, silently demanding an explanation. When one wasn't immediately offered, he asked: "What the fuck happened?"

Kaymel shook his head from side to side while taking a deep breath. Then before Steve had a chance to ask anymore questions, Kaymel dropped the bomb.

"Green eyes is dead. He got killed last night outside of Gordon's.

CHAPTER 7

Murder! Jeff was locked up for murder! For a moment Tasia was in denial. There had to be some kind of mistake because Jeff would never kill anyone, unless... no! Jeff was smarter than that. And, he knew all too well the wisdom of thinking for the next man. But the fact remained, Jeff was in jail accused of taking the life of another human being.

After Tasia got off the phone with Jeff, she called Jeff's mother like he had asked her to do. Mrs. Wilson was half asleep and not happy to be receiving a call at almost 11 o'clock at night. When Tasia identified herself and Mrs. Wilson perceived apprehension in her tone, Jeff's mom immediately became alert.

"Child, is everything okay? Oh Lord..." Mrs. Wilson's intuition immediately kicked in.

Jeff's mom, like any other mom, dreaded the sound of the phone ringing in the middle of the night because it usually signified trouble.

"Ma, Jeff got locked up last night." Tasia said, and that's when the reality hit her like a ton of bricks.

"Locked up? What on earth-"

"He's locked up for murder," Tasia broke down and started crying, "He said he didn't do it but the judge still didn't give him a bail, Now I don't know what to do, I'm out here all by myself-"

"Wait a minute Tasia, try to calm down. Murder? Who they saying my baby killed? And if he got locked up last night, then why on earth are you just calling me?"

"It's just so much going on and I didn't know what to do. All I know is Jeff's friend Antwon came home from the war-"

"-Okay, I know who Antwon is, go ahead baby"

"So Jeff said they were just going out for drinks because Antwon was only on leave for a week. Then I couldn't sleep because Jeff never came home..." Tasia was crying so hard by now that she was having a hard time speaking.

"Lord have Mercy. So you don't know who they're saying he killed?"

"No." Tasia managed to say between sniffles.

"Okay, listen to me baby. You need to be strong right now. If the good lord sees fit to test my baby, then he has a right to do so, but we need to have faith! Jonah was swallowed by a whale and he still had faith, and the Lord set him free. So you be strong Tasia, and pray, that's all we can do now is pray. It's in the hands of the Lord, do you understand?"

"Yes maam."

"Now, where are they holding my baby??"

"He's on Rikers Island. He has a visit tomorrow so I'm going to take him some underclothes and something to wear to court. I have to try and find him a lawyer too."

"Do you need any money? I can go to the bank in the morning."

"No Ma, we have some money put away. I should be able to keep it together for a little while, at least until we can clear Jeff's name."

Tasia was feeling a bit more optimistic now. Jeff's mom was right, everything was in God's hands.

"Well, what time is the visit?"

"Six o'clock in the evening"

"Good, I'll be ready by five."

Tasia was deprived of sleep for nearly 48 hours, so when she finally hit the sack she slept like a grizzly. It's amazing what proper rest could do for a person. Tasia woke up energized and ready to go! She packed a bag with socks, under wear, and three outfits so Jeff would have a change of clothes and something appropriate to wear to court.

She then searched on line for a decent criminal attorney, and after surfing the world wide web for almost an hour, Tasia was ready to start making some phone calls.

After setting up an appointment to meet with Dale Slotnick at 10 a.m., Tasia stopped by the bank and withdrew $5,000 just in case the lawyer required a retainer. By the time she was seated in the spacious offices of Slotnick and Associates, which was directly across the street from the Criminal Court Building on Queens boulevard, Mr. Slotnick had all the information he needed pertaining to Jeff's case.

"Ms. Brown, I've been working the phone lines all morning. I've already spoken to the Assistant District Attorney assigned to your boyfriends case, as well as the arresting officers..," Mr. Slotnick took off his glasses and began to massage his temples, "And to be frank with you, I'm not going to be able to take this case."

Tasia appeared to be confused.

"Why not? I mean, I came way down here-"

"Ms. Brown, I apologize for your inconvenience, but, the fact of the matter is that your boyfriend doesn't have a defense. A man was killed, and your boyfriend was caught at the scene of the crime with the murder weapon. Had I known that when I spoke to you earlier I could've saved you a trip."

Tasia's heartbeat quickened and she suddenly felt as if she was on the verge of an anxiety attack.

"No! Jeff is innocent! I spoke to him myself and he told me that he didn't do it. Even if he did have the murder weapon, which I don't believe, that doesn't mean that he killed anybody. How many witnesses do they have?"

Mr. Slotnick took a deep breath, but he certainly appeared to be amused.

"There are no witnesses, and you're right, just because he was caught with the weapon, red handed, that doesn't necessarily mean that he's guilty. But you have to admit, it's pretty darned conclusive. What lawyer in his right mind would try this case in front of a jury? They'll convict him without ever leaving the court room to deliberate. If your boyfriend is smart he'll take a plea, because if he's found guilty the judge will sentence him to 25 years to life in prison."

'Relax Tasia, this is just a bad dream. This is not real.' Tasia thought.

"Well, how much time would he get if he was to take a plea?"

"My guess... with a case like this, 15 years to life."

Tasia shook her head from side to side in a gesture to say *You've got to be kidding me!*

"What the hell is the difference between 15 to life and 25 to life?" Tasia asked sarcastically.

Mr. Slotnick smiled, a sympathetic smile.

"If he blows trial . . . he'll find out in the sixteenth year."

Modular six in C-74 consisted of two sides; a north side and a south side. Each side had the capacity to hold up to fifty prisoners in a large dormitory structure that boasted a bathroom and shower area, living quarters, and a dayroom for recreational purposes. A row of one man bunks hugged the walls in the living quarters while two back to back rows of beds settled in the middle allowing a small aisle to run full circle through the sleeping area.

On the south side of modular six, despite fatigue, Jeff was having a hard time falling asleep. Besides the murder charge weighing heavily on his mind, the guys who lived in his section of the dorm were hosting an after dark talent contest. These guys seemed oblivious to the fact that they were in jail. They were doing standup comedy, rapping and singing their favorite songs, and if that wasn't bad enough, the guys who were able to sleep through the show were either snoring loudly or letting out silent but deadly farts that forced some of the guys to seek refuge under their blankets.

Rondu was up at the front of the dorm kicking it to a red bone female officer that had a nice ass but an out of control acne problem. Almost all of the officers knew or at least heard of Rondu and it seemed as if his reputation alone afforded him V.I.P. treatment.

Never the less, Jeff was relieved when Rondu finally decided to get some shut eye, because, dude was not having all that noise. When the Craig Mack looking chick was relieved by a male officer, Rondu pulled the plug on the late night talent show.

"Aiight, ya'll niggaz might as well go to sleep 'cause it's quiet time! All that fake 50 cent, R.Kelly wanna-be bullshit is dead! Think it's a joke if ya'll want, violators will be prosecuted, and I'm the mutha fuckin' judge in this bitch"

Rondu proceeded to get ready for bed and the only response he received was the sound of light snoring and an occasional fart. Rondu went to go brush his teeth and when he came back in the sleeping area on his way to his bed, he slapped the shit out of the dude in the bed next to his.

"Hmm Yo! what happened?!?" The guy said coming out of a deep sleep.

"You snoring, nigga, that's what the fuck happened! Turn over and lay on your stomach or something-- it's quiet time!" Rondu barked and then waited to see if ole boy had a problem before getting in his bed.

After that, Jeff slept like a baby. He was so tired he slept past breakfast, and when he finally woke up, one of the first things he noticed was that his sneakers were gone. Someone stole his white on white Air Force ones!

Jeff sat up in bed and studied his surroundings. Some guys were still sleeping but the majority could be seen in the dayroom crowded around the television. Jeff opened the small locker that was next to his bed and saw the famous Rikers Island green cup, his toothbrush and tooth paste and the inmate rules and regulations handbook that they gave him in the receiving room. He closed the locker and looked under the bed, but, his sneakers were no where to be found.

A dark skin kid with shoulder length dread locks was a few beds down looking out the window while he listened to his walkman. He was bobbing his head to the music and spitting the lyrics of the song out loud seemingly in his own little world until he noticed Jeff was woke.

"Oh shit! My bad son, I woke you up?" the dude asked as he removed his headphones from his ears.

"Nah, you good." Jeff said nonchalantly.

Dude was looking at Jeff hard, as if Jeff looked familiar and dude was trying to figure out where he knew him from.

"Where you from, son?"

Jeff wasn't in the mood to be interrogated but at the same time he wasn't looking for trouble.

"I'm from Queens."

Dude crunched his face up. "What part?"

"Jamaica,"

"Word? I know a shorty that lives in Jamaica! Her name is Lorraine, she from Merrick Boulevard over there by I.S.8, you know her?"

"Lorraine?" Jeff asked.

"Yeah, she got a daughter name Asia"

"Nah, I know a chick name Lorraine but she don't got no kids. The Lorraine I know is dark skin, she got burn marks on her face."

"Word?" dude said nodding his head, "What's your name, son?"

"Jeff!"

"Alright Jeff, everybody calls me Dread. I'm from Bed

Stuy, ya heard? You got a couple of cats in here from Queens."

"Yeah aiight. I'm about to get myself together Dread, I'll holla at you in a minute." Jeff said as he went inside his locker and grabbed his toothbrush and toothpaste.

Before Jeff could go and take care of his hygiene, Dread walked over and dropped some worn down looking Reeboks on Jeff's bed.

"You hear me, son?" Dread said cracking his Knuckles. "Put those on for now, 'cause I know you're not trying to walk around here bare foot. They're a little raggedy, but as soon as something decent come through you got first dibs, ya heard?"

Jeff looked at the dirty Reeboks on his bed and then back at Dread. It dawned on him immediately, *'this nigga got my sneakers.'*

"Where my shit at, Dread?" Jeff asked standing up to confront ole boy.

That's when the door to the dayroom opened briefly, giving freedom to 50 Cent's song *'I get money'* that blasted from the television. Two dudes came out of the dayroom and approached the living quarters.

"Dread, what's good my nigga?" one of the dudes said posting up near Dread.

The other guy that came out of the day room sat on a locker nearby so he could have a ring side seat when the drama unfolded.

"Aint shit, Born! Somebody took son sneakers." Dread said with a smirk, never breaking eye contact with Jeff.

The kid Born spit out a gem star razor blade that he carried around in his mouth.

"What? somebody stole your sneakers?" Born asked Jeff

as if he was indignant, "Who you think got your shit my nigga, pick a herb!"

Jeff didn't believe he was going through this bullshit. These dudes were playing him like a cold blooded lame. Jeff silently wondered what he had done to deserve this.

He turned his attention to the dude name Born, "Man, I just want my sneakers back, all that other shit aint about nothing."

The door to the dayroom opened and closed again. This time it was Rondu coming, and he smelled drama in the air.

"What the fuck is up? Niggaz trying to get it in? Cause if so ya'll can skip the formalities with all of that staring shit and get it the fuck poppin'!"

"Somebody stole my nigga sneakers," Born said deceitfully.

"Somebody stole? Oh hell no, we don't do no stealing up in this bitch! That aint gangsta! If a nigga gonna rob a nigga he gotta do that shit straight up! Fuck all that faggot shit, sneak thieves will be prosecuted-- and I'm the mutha fucking judge! Now, who got that nigga shit?" Rondu said.

Rondu walked back to the day room and pulled the plug on the T.V. before coming back to the sleeping area.

"We gonna get to the bottom of this shit! Now who the fuck is the individual, or individuals, who stole a niggas sneakers?" Rondu yelled.

Everybody started to file out of the dayroom to see what Rondu was tripping about. A few people who were still in bed were now sitting up to see what all the commotion was about.

"Don't make me play court in this bitch, I'll go through every locker in here, and then I'm taking the guilty party to trial. Think it's a joke until I sentence a mutha fucker to a severe ass whippin'!"

Dread went to his locker and pulled out Jeff's sneakers.

"I got his sneakers, son! Me and that nigga can shoot five for them," Dread said walking to the back of the dorm with the sneakers.

To shoot five meant to fight head up for five minutes, although no one actually kept track of the time.

"Oh hell no, it's too late for that now Dread! You's a grimey mutha fucker, NO I'm lying, I'M a grimey mutha fucker-- niggaz like you are worse than grimey. You's a petty ass sneak thief—"

"Nigga it's whatever, I aint no fuckin' sneak thief!" Dread finally declared, deciding not to duck rec.

Rondu jumped off the locker he was sitting on and started walking toward the back where Dread was, "Do I sense resistance? I was gonna be nice and give you a fair trial, but now..."

Dread threw up his hands in defense as Rondu approached.

"Your ass is," Rondu commenced to whipping Dread's ass, "Guilty!"

Rondu rained blows on dude until he was balled up on the floor trying to block and cover his face, and then he started stomping a mud hole in his ass.

"You's a petty ass nigga and you better be lucky I don't kill your mutha fucking ass," Rondu hollered as he exerted himself, "Born, that's your man?" Rondu asked advancing toward ole boy who had the razor in his mouth.

"I came to jail by myself-- fuck that petty ass nigga!" Born said with the quickness.

Rondu turned back around and picked up the sneakers before walking over and tossing them on Jeff's bed.

"I'm telling ya'll niggaz now . . . if you got sticky fingers and you get caught stealing, I'm trying my best to break your mutha fucking hands! If somebody got something you want that bad-- call the nigga out and shoot five for it. Be a fucking man about it! And Born, ya'll pack that nigga Dread's shit, he gotta go. Send that nigga to the north side or something, because if he get in my way I'm gonna try to tear his head off!"

After that, the case was closed. Jeff had his sneakers back and Dread was transferred to another housing unit. That just goes to show you . . . even in the belly of the beast-- there's a method to the madness.

CHAPTER 8

Someone had killed Green Eyes and it was Steve's job to find and deal with whoever was responsible.

Being that Doonie and Blast was the last ones with Green Eyes, those were the people that Steve wanted to talk to first. He told them to meet him in Forty projects; the heart of South Jamaica, Queens, where the crew primarily conducted their illegal business.

Driving up 160th street, Steve spotted and parked behind Doonies grey Dodge Magnum which was double parked on 109th avenue right across the street from 40 park.

Charlie Brown, JuJu, and Slow Berry were in a heated dice game right there on the corner while foot soldiers inconspicuously sold packages of crack cocaine within the vicinity.

Steve observed the terrain with the eye of a military commander, acknowledging those worthy of acknowledgement with a slight nod of his head as he made his way over to where Doonie and Blast were posted up.

"What up?" Steve asked with a straight face as he continued to study the block.

"Aint shit! We were just waiting on you." Doonie responded.

Steve gave them both some dap and then got right down

to business.

"Yo, what happened? Yall already know that Kaymel is madder than a mutha fucker that ya'll didn't tell nobody where yall was going. Then to top it off yall got caught slipping, one of yall please tell me what the fuck happened."

"Steve listen," Blast started. He took a couple of deep breaths before he continued," You already know how Green Eyes is. I love that nigga and the whole nine but Steve, you know how he is! I didn't wanna go to no damn strip club, that's ya'll thing-- no disrespect. Green Eyes is the one who wanted to go, so we went! The joint was crazy crowded and a nigga accidentally bumped into Green Eyes, it was an accident Steve! Green Eyes blew the whole thing out of proportion. He died over some bullshit!" Blast said, tears running freely down his face.

"We tried to dead that shit, because for real-for real it wasn't about nothing." Doonie added, but, Blast wasn't finished.

"When we left the club, Green Eyes told us to hold up, he was talking to somebody on his cell phone. So we was chillin' by the truck, and I swear on my mother's grave I knew this nigga was stalling. I knew he was waiting on them niggaz to come out the club. I just looked at Doonie and shook my head. Doonie already had the desert eagle out the stash box and I had my nine so we wasn't slipping . . . but that shit happened so fast."

Steve listened to their whole story and then questioned both of them thoroughly. Afterward, he was convinced that there was nothing that Doonie nor Blast could've done to prevent what happened to Green Eyes.

The break through came when Steve went to see Green Eyes's mother. She was holding up pretty well and she seemed to be in good spirits after receiving what she deemed to be good news. The police had arrested someone in connection to her son's death. The arrest wouldn't bring Green Eyes back, but, to his loved ones it did provide a small degree of relief.

Steve knew that Kaymel would be happy about the latest development, because now they had a name. Jeffery Wilson! Jeffery Wilson was responsible for killing Green Eyes.

CHAPTER 9

Jeff brushed his teeth and took a much needed long hot shower. When he returned to his bed he was happy to see his sneakers exactly where he had left them. The loud mouth dude from the bus, Rondu, turned, out to be a blessing in disguise.

Still, many of the inmates in the dorm began to despise Jeff. They felt that he was less than a man because he didn't fight his own battle, and consequently the people had little or no respect for him.

Jeff saw the smirks and open stares he received from the other inmates but he pretty much ignored it all. His motto was: *'As long as nobody put their hands on me.'*

The way Jeff looked at it, he had far more important things to worry about, such as his relationship with Tasia, his job at Modell's market, and last but not least trying to exonerate himself from the homicide he was charged with. As imposing as that all may have seemed, it was still vital for Jeff to acclimate to his new environment.

"Get ready for chow!" a lanky male officer announced, alerting the dorm that it was time for lunch, "And the following inmates pack your things because you'll be moving,"

The officer proceeded to call seven names from the list he held, and a wave of excitement shot through the dorm. Mod six was temporary housing for new inmates, and as such, the atmosphere was constantly changing. All types of criminals came and went, and consequently so did the drama as was demonstrated through the situation with Dread. But for the most part Mod six was sweet in comparison to the rest of the population. The dorms and other cell blocks throughout C-74 were more established and filled with horror stories. Rikers Island itself was a place where only the strong survived. Cowards were forced to wash peoples clothes by hand, give up choice food in the prison mess hall (especially chicken), and they only used the telephone when absolutely no one else was able to use it, and even then they needed permission from another inmate. They couldn't sit down and watch television in the dayroom even though some guys would be sitting on five or six chairs stacked up on each other, so they would just sort of linger around in the back. The #1 rule for cowards was to stay the hell out the way! So most cowards did their best to become invisible.

This being the reality, it was understandable why some people would've preferred to stay in Mod six, even the guys who would ultimately hold their own was in no rush to go to population.

Jeff looked over and saw Born, the same guy that carried a razor blade in his mouth, dumping all of his property onto a blanket he had spread out on the floor. This was how people traveled on the island, they would wrap all of their belongings in sheets or blankets and drag them from point A to point B.

Born didn't look too happy to be leaving but, he wore a mask of deception for his peers that crowded around him.

"South side, on the chow!" the lanky officer yelled, and everyone began to file out into the hallway.

The guys who were leaving were instructed to bring their

property along with them, so there were seven guys at the back of the line with all of their belongings tied up in blankets.

"Deuce it up, fellas!" The officer commanded before quickly taking a count. There were forty-eight bodies on the south side of Mod six.

"O'kay, listen up... Brown, Harris, and Cox," the officer said looking at the floor cards in his hand and then at the faces at the back of the line, "You're going to 4 upper! We eat first so we'll drop you off on the way and you guys will eat with your unit . . . Davis, you're going to 4 main, Allen and Richards-- Mod nine, and King you'll be going to Mod seven. Gentlemen, I know I don't need to remind you-- don't drop the soap! South side, take it up the stairs and stay in formation."

It was like a cow run! The inmates mostly did what they were expected to do. In two lines they filed out into the huge corridor that expanded through the even side of the building. C-74 was comprised of two sides; an even side and an odd side. The even side consisted of the even number cell blocks and the odd side consisted of the odd number cell blocks.

Rondu was easily the livest dude on the south side of Mod six, and as such he commandeered the front of the line with another kid named Nitty who was representing Brooklyn. "Gentlemen, take it down to the next line." The C.O instructed.

There were red lines on the floor about every 75 feet designed to control the flow of traffic in the corridor. When the group arrived at their first stop they were near the entrance that led to 4 main, 4 upper, and 4 lower, The C.O. called out the four names of the guys being dropped at that destination and they fell out of the line dragging their belongings with them.

"Don't forget what I said about the soap," the C.O.

laughed handing them their floor cards which included pertinent information on them along with a photograph of the inmate it represented, "Give your floor card to the officer on your unit. South side, take it down to the next line, and gentlemen, no talking in my hallways."

Jeff couldn't believe he was actually in jail. He was in denial, but all of his senses were screaming: "This is real, this is not a test!"

When they made it to the next line they were near the entrance that led to modulars seven, eight, and nine. There was a chocolate sister wearing a glove fitting uniform jingling the keys to the door.

"Williams, what are you doing back here?" She asked Rondu as if she was deeply concerned.

"You already know, shit happens." Rondu responded. The lanky officer escorting the unit to chow called off the remaining names and gave their floor cards to the female officer.

"How's it going Ms. Smith? I got three for you."

The three guys dragged their property and filed through the door that would lead them to their new residences.

"I'm doing great, Foster, how about yourself?" Ms Smith asked with a smile.

"I can, but I'm not complaining. South side take it down!"

As the guys walked past Ms Smith, almost no one was able to resist staring at her banging body-- even Jeff was taken back.

"Damn!" somebody said a little too loud.

"And you can thank the jack ass who said that for the T.V. being off when we get back to the unit. The day room will be closed for an hour, does anyone want to make it two hours?" CO Foster challenged.

When no one responded, they proceeded to the even side mess hall without incident.

Tasia and Jeff's mom took the F train to Queens plaza and then caught the city bus to Rikers Island. When they got off the bus at the last stop, they had to wait for a bus from the Department of Corrections to take them across the formidable bridge that led to the residence of despair and loneliness.

As they were being processed, the harsh reality of what was happening was overwhelming and Tasia broke down and started crying. It caught Mrs. Wilson off guard because they were just talking about how high the price of gas was and Tasia seemed to be fine.

"God is in control, baby, we just need to have faith." Mrs. Wilson said as she grabbed and held Tasia's hand "Every thing is going to be okay"

"I know, Ma. It's just that Jeff Is all by himself." Tasia cried.

"The Lord is with him, baby. We're never alone."

Visitors were being loaded onto specific buses and transported to the numerous buildings on Rikers Island, but those in route to C-74 only had to walk across the Street to the Adolescent Reception Detention Center (A.R.D.C).

Tasia willed herself to be strong. Life was filled with obstacles and challenges, and this was just the latest edition. She held her head high and mentally prepared to be strong for her man.

CHAPTER 10

Shakim was a cruddy dude, but, he was convinced that some women were even more cruddier than niggaz. Although Sha participated in high risk sexual activities on a daily basis he still found it hard to believe that one of his chicks gave him the heebie jeebies. He was convinced that it was either Shelly or Tamika, and even though he suspected the latter, there was no doubt that he would make both of their nasty butts pay.

Presently Shakim was laying low in his 1995 black Nissan maxima with illegal tinted windows, and he was creeping through the hood. He just finished dropping his man Boogie off in Red fern projects, Far Rockaway, and now he was headed back to the south side of Jamaica, Queens.

Lately Sha found himself looking for reasons to hang out with Boogie. Whenever the two of them got together they would smoke blunts of weed laced with crack cocaine, a mixture they called woolies, woolahs, or just plain ole woos. At first it was just weed. Then one day while Boogie was riding shot gun in the Range Rover he lit up a blunt and refused to pass it to Sha.

"Pass the blunt, Boogie, damn man!"

Boogie was holding in smoke as he looked at Sha through the haze of smoke, "Shit, you don't want none of this."

"True story, if you don't pass that blunt your ass is gonna

be walking home."

"It's laced!" Boogie said breathing smoke through his nostrils.

About the same time as he said it, Shakim caught the familiar sweet smell of cocaine in the air. Sha use to smoke cigarettes laced with cocaine back in the days but it was a phase he was able to overcome,

"Nigga, you smoking crack up in my shit?" Sha spit.

Boogie was dragging hard on the blunt.

"Man, you wanna hit this shit or not?" Boogie asked holding in the smoke as he held out the blunt for Sha.

Sha took his eyes off the road for a quick second and glanced at the smoking blunt.

"That shit do smell good," he said snatching the woolie from Boogie, "Don't be making this no habit, crack head, plain weed is cool with me."

That was two months ago! Since then Sha found himself hooking up with Boogie more and more, and every time they hooked up they smoked woos.

Now Sha drove slowly down Union hall street until he spotted Tamika and her girl friends sitting on a stoop in front of a pink house.

Inside the ash tray was three perfectly rolled blunts of weed laced with crack. Sha was developing a habit although he was reluctant to admit it, and today he planned to turn Tamika on to his new high. If she would just follow his lead her dumb ass would be a crack head in no time, Sha thought, and it would serve her right for giving him VD, if she was the one who in fact gave it to him.

Sha rolled down the passenger side window and waved

at Tamikas friends.

"Hi Shakim!" they said, smiling and trying to flirt on the low.

Sha wanted to fuck every last one of them except for maybe Michelle who was damn near 300 pounds. If he was high enough he'd smash her fat ass too.

"How ya'll ladies doing?" Sha said smoothly as Tamika came and slid into the passenger seat.

"If I had your hand Shakim, I would cut mine off." One of the girls named Donetta said with a seductive look that spoke volumes.

"Yeah, and if I was you, I'd probably do the same thing." Sha responded arrogantly.

"I know that's right!" Tamika said, happy that Shakim just shitted on Donetta's hating ass.

As Sha pulled off, he passed Tamika his lighter, "Go ahead and light one of them blunts up."

CHAPTER 11

"Wilson… Jeffrey Wilson, you have a visit" The C.O. yelled before sitting back down to finish polishing her finger nails.

Jeff had been lying on his bunk in a zone and he quickly got up to prepare for his visit.

The first thing he did was grab his tooth brush and tooth paste before rushing to brush his teeth.

Rondu didn't miss nothing! "That's you they called for a visit?" he asked with the inquisitiveness of a child. Jeff nodded his head in the affirmative.

"Here, don't use that bullshit toothpaste, it makes your breath stink. I got some official shit for you." Rondu said grabbing a tube of Aqua Fresh from atop his locker.

Rondu had came up on a decent supply of necessities after running around in the hallways when the institution allowed the inmates to freely move to medical in order to receive their prescribed medication. He went to Mod eight and hollered at his homies Courtney and Waturi, he went to Mod nine and kicked it with Jeff dogg, and he snuck up to 4 upper and chilled with Freeze for about a half an hour. By the time he finished making his rounds he had a pillow case filled with all types of commissary items, a thick Cuban link gold chain with a cross medallion, and a balloon stuffed with some strawberry hydro that was so potent that you could smell it even while it was concealed in Rondu's pocket.

"Good looking out," Jeff said as he accepted the toothpaste.

Rondu followed him to the bathroom.

"You smoke?" he asked Jeff.

Jeff paused while brushing his teeth and shook his head to say no.

"You don't fuck with trees?" Rondu asked incredulously. Jeff spit into the sink and said "Oh, you talking about weed, I thought you was talking about cigarettes. Yeah I blow once in a while."

"When you get back, I got you." Rondu said feeling him out.

When Jeff was ready to leave for his visit, Rondu loaned him a pair of Fila slippers. A grey or brown jumpsuit and slippers was what inmates were required to wear in the visiting room.

A number of inmates were paying close attention to Jeff now, although they pretended not to be. If he was going on a visit that meant he had people that cared for him, and it also meant he might be able to make some moves; smuggle drugs into the facility.

Jeff was oblivious to the fact that he had just become popular. The C.O. electronically popped the lock from inside the control bubble, and Jeff was out the door.

The visiting room was a large open area with small tables situated in rows. A murmur resonated throughout the room as inmates conversated with family and friends in an attempt at maintaining ties with the outside world.

Tasia and Mrs. Wilson were escorted into the visiting room by a young African American male sporting shoulder length dreadlocks and gold teeth. Tasia noticed the look in the officer's eyes whenever he spoke to her, and she even caught him staring at her butt a few times. Tasia was use to this kind of attention but she hardly expected it under the circumstances. But then again, she remembered when she was at her cousin's funeral and a guy named Gary had the audacity to try to push up on her at a time when she was paying respect.

After they were seated, the officer made his rounds walking around the visiting room, every now and then he tried to make eye contact with Tasia. Tasia politely batted down the subtle advances and concentrated on the door that the inmates were using to enter the visiting room.

After about fifteen minutes, ole boy with the dreadlocks stopped by the table.

"It's normal for the guys to take this long coming down. You know they have to take a shower and all of that good stuff, but, if he's not here within the next 10 minutes or so I'll call his unit again to see what's the hold up."

"God bless your soul. Thank you kindly sir, we sure do appreciate it." Mrs. Wilson said.

"No problem, maam." the officer responded before turning his attention to Tasia, "Don't I know you from somewhere? I mean, you look real familiar." He was looking at Tasia with a smile and lust in his eyes.

"No, I don't think so." Tasia said curtly.

"Where you from?" Ole boy prodded boldly.

Tasia started to check dude, but, thankfully she glanced up and saw Jeff coming into the visiting room with a group of inmates.

"Look ma, there go Jeff!" Tasia said standing up and silently dismissing the intrusion.

Mrs. Wilson who was outwardly the strong link, covered her face with her hands and began to cry when she saw her son approaching the table wearing a brown jump suit and red, white and blue Fila slippers. Her shoulders began to shake up and down, and the sight alone filled Jeff's heart with sorrow.

Jeff gave Tasia a smothering hug before standing in front of the woman who was partly responsible for his existence. He put his hands on her shoulders, gently massaging them.

"I'm alright mommy, come on, you know better than I do that everything is going to be fine." Jeff said soothingly.

"Yeah, Ma, don't cry," Tasia added sitting next to her mother in law and placing a hand on her back, "God is in control. At the end of the day everything is in His hands."

Mrs. Wilson wiped at her tears and looked up at Jeff with years of pain and suffering in her eyes. She stood up and embraced her son as if they would never see each other again.

Jeff held his mother tightly while looking at Tasia over her shoulder. He kept repeating: "It's going to be okay."

Even as he spoke the words, Jeff didn't know what to expect. Presently, his future was looking so dim that at times he wondered how he would make it without going crazy. Still, he knew he needed to be strong, if not for him, then for his mother and Tasia.

Reluctantly he broke the embrace and took his seat on the other side of the table. All inmates had to sit across from their visitors.

"What took you so long to come down?" Tasia asked pretending to have an attitude.

"I came as soon as they called me. How long was y'all waiting?"

"It wasn't that bad," Tasia said looking at Jeff with her lip poked out, "How are you feeling?"

That was the million dollar question . . . how did he feel? Jeff was scared, lonely, tired, and confused, and he felt like shit but he definitely didn't need his family worrying themselves sick over his predicament.

"I'm good, Boo. I'm just trying to maintain positive thoughts... I'm not gonna lie and say it's not difficult, but, you know my mama didn't raise no punk." Jeff said looking at his mother with a smile.

"Baby, they feeding you in here? What's the food like?" Mrs. Wilson asked with great concern.

"I've only been here for a couple of days Ma, but the food is alright. It's nothing to write home about."

"Anybody bothering you in there? Do you know anybody?" Mrs. Wilson asked.

Jeff thought about the situation with his sneakers.

"I wish somebody would mess with me, Ma. What's your favorite saying when somebody wants trouble?"

Mrs. Wilson was confused at first, then she smiled at the memory of one of the lessons in life that she dispersed to her children, "You have to bring ass to get ass!" she said reverting to her younger days. She always taught her boys if someone hits them, pick up something and go up against somebody's head.

"I know that's right." Tasia said and then continued,

"Baby, what happened? I talked to a lawyer today and he gave me the District Attorney's version of what happened but I want to hear it from you."

Mrs. Wilson was all ears, and Jeff noticed the C.O. with the dreads looking all in his mouth but he thought nothing of it. He took a deep breath and recapped everything that happened on that fateful night. Of course Jeff left out the part about him being intimate with Tropical.

Never the less, Tasia was fuming! If Jeff was innocent, then why in hell was he sitting in jail? Tasia couldn't fathom why Jeff didn't tell the police that Chip was the one who killed the guy. As a matter of fact, Tasia wanted to know why wasn't Chip being 21 about the whole situation and holding his own weight as opposed to allowing Jeff to take the fall?

"This is messed up. I don't believe this, Jeff. So, now you're living by the code of the street? You're just going to sit back and take the blame and do 25 to life for something you didn't do?" Tasia asked.

Mrs. Wilson felt the same way but didn't know how to articulate what she was feeling.

"I'm not going to do no 25 to life, Boo, and I'm not taking the blame. I'm going to fight the charge--- I'm innocent." Jeff said as if it was that simple.

Tasia couldn't believe that the man that she loved was being so darned naive. She sucked her teeth, "Nigga! They caught you with the smoking gun!"

"Tasia! Mrs. Wilson said placing her hand on Tasia's arm.

"I'm sorry Ma, but he's not making any sense." Tasia said, her voice strong yet emotional.

"Jeff, Tasia is right, these people are going to try to lock you up for the rest of your life." Mrs. Wilson said holding her heart, "My heart is not strong enough for that, baby, please, just tell them people exactly what happened like you just told us."

Jeff just sat there quietly. He had no intentions of snitching on Chip.

"Do you hear your mother talking to you, Jeff?"

"I hear her."

"Well, don't just sit there, say something!" Tasia said hotly.

Still, Jeff remained silent. He was ashamed that his loved ones had to endure such foolishness. In his heart, Jeff felt that he was doing the right thing. If he didn't appreciate being locked up and charged with murder, then why would he cause the next man to be in that same predicament?

While Jeff continued to be silent, Tasia sucked her teeth and turned her chair away so she wasn't facing him.

"Jeffrey, who is Chip? Is he a good friend, is that why you're protecting him?" Jeff's mom asked.

"You know Chip," Jeff said and then continued, "He use to come to the house back in the days. He was on my basketball team."

"You're not talking about the little big head boy with the chipped tooth in his mouth, are you?" Mrs. Wilson asked.

"Yeah, that's him."

"Oh Lord, that boy done went and killed somebody." Mrs. Wilson said theatrically.

Tasia looked at Jeff and rolled her eyes.

"Don't be like that, Boo, not now, I need you." Jeff said.

"If you need me, then you'll do what you need to do to come home to me." Tasia said, but she loosened up a bit because she knew that Jeff did need her, especially at that point.

Just then the officer with the dreadlocks came and pointed at the row that they were sitting in, "Everyone in this row, your time is up. Please say your goodbyes and proceed to the front of the visiting room. Inmates remain seated."

Jeff gave Tasia and his mom, big hugs, and he Blessed Tasia with a deep passionate kiss.

"Ya'll get home safe, I love ya'll!" Jeff said.

"Love you too, son, and be careful in there."

"You know I love you, Boo! If you can, call me, and um.... don't drop the soap." Tasia said with a wicked smile.

Then they were gone, and once again Jeff was all alone.

CHAPTER 12

When Tasia made it home from visiting Jeff she was overcome by ambivalence. She was happy that she was finally able to see Jeff and to know that he was alive and well, but at the same time she was saddened by the insurmountable trial that they were faced with.

'He is so stubborn' Tasia thought as she recalled their conversation.

As far as she was concerned, Jeff was willing to sacrifice his own life for some no good negro. Tasia knew if the shoe were on the other foot that Chip would've gave Jeff up in a heartbeat.

As Tasia kicked off her shoes a selfish thought crossed her mind. Among other things, Tasia was concerned about the good loving she'd grown accustomed to receiving on a daily basis. Sure she had discipline, but she knew she'd be lying if she didn't admit that Jeff's absence was going to create one hell of a void. If worse came to worse she could always please herself, plus she could purchase a few toys to add some excitement, but, what about when she needed someone to hold her at night? what about companionship? And how would she prepare herself for the worst case scenario?

After taking a bath and preparing a simple dinner of Ramen Noodles, Tasia checked her messages and began returning calls. First she called Alan, Jeff's boss at Modell's market, and she explained to him why Jeff wasn't and wouldn't be coming to work. Alan was shocked to learn that Jeff was in jail but he immediately offered to help in anyway he could.

Not only was Jeff a good worker, but, Alan also considered him a friend. Before hanging up he assured Tasia that when the misunderstanding was cleared up and Jeff was released, his job would still be waiting for him.

Next Tasia called Sean Howard, a real estate broker, to reschedule an appointment she had to cancel due to the situation with Jeff. Sean had a client that was interested in an income property on Hillside Avenue that Tasia was handling on behalf of Colossal Realty. Tasia was eager to close the deal because at the end of the day she stood to gain a huge commission.

Sean Howard agreed to reschedule for the very next day at 1 p.m.

Finally, before calling it a night, Tasia called her mom.

"Hello." her mother answered nonchalantly as if she didn't see her daughter's name on the caller I.D.

"Hi ma, I'm sorry for calling so late but I had an emergency," Tasia said in way of an apology.

"An emergency? What in the world-- is everything o'kay?"

Tasia knew that her mother was a certified gossip monger, and she was skeptical about sharing her business with her. But then again, she knew her mom would find out sooner or later about the situation with Jeff so she just decided to come clean.

"Ma, Jeff is in jail. I was running around all day trying to get him a decent lawyer, and I'm just getting in from Rikers island."

There was silence on the line as Tasia's mom digested the news.

"I'm telling you because I trust you," Tasia added, using child psychology and knowing good and well it was useless because her mother had a big mouth, she continued, "and I don't want you telling anybody-"

"No, no, no, I aint telling nobody shit! What's the Vegetable man doing in jail? He killed somebody?" Tasia's mom whispered in a conspiratorial tone.

Because Jeff worked at a produce market, Tasia's mom dubbed him the vegetable man.

"Someone was shooting outside the club and a guy was killed, now they're trying to say that Jeff did it." Tasia said keeping the story as simple as possible.

"Whaaaat?" Tasia's mom dragged the word, indicating this was the juiciest piece of information she'd heard in a long while. "Well, why they think Jeff did it?" She continued as if the whole thing made absolutely no sense.

"Because Jeff was there when it happened."

"What in the world was the vegetable man doing at, never mind, who are they saying he killed? Anybody I know?"

"No Ma! And I'm serious, I don't want my business in the street-"

"Child, I heard you! Who am I going to tell? You act like you're the mother and I'm the child."

"I'm just saying, Ma . . . listen, I have to go, you know I have to go to work in the morning. I love you and I'll keep you posted."

"Yeah, you do that, and I love you too Tasia!"

Tasia turned her phone off and plugged her charger in.

The road ahead of her would be long and tough, and Tasia knew she would need all the rest she could get, so she went straight to bed. Alone. Again. Without Jeff.

It was comedy night at Manhattan Proper, a hole in the wall club on Linden boulevard in the Cambria Heights section of Queens. Shakim and Stephanie had a table not too far away from the small stage.

Every once in a while Sha would sneak off somewhere with Stephanie, usually somewhere remote so he didn't risk being seen in public with ole girl. It wasn't that Stephanie was bad looking, Shakim just didn't want people getting the wrong idea.

But this night was different! On this occasion Sha sported Stephanie on his arm like a trophy and they were right there around the way. This was Shakim's way of apologizing to Stephanie for giving her gonorrhea.

While he wasn't in a rush to get serious with Stephanie, Sha had to admit she was a good girl. Steph always had his back regardless of him being right or wrong, even when he was broke. And Stephanie was one of the few people he could be himself around, with her there were no pretentions.

That's why Sha felt obligated to tell Stephanie that it would be a good idea for her to go see the doctor. At first, Stephanie had been confused, she didn't understand what Sha was trying to convey. But once he spelled it out for her, Stephanie was livid!

"What do you mean you're burning?" She screamed,

"You're out there sticking your little dick in anything with two legs and you don't have enough sense to protect yourself?"

Sha started to remind her that the two of them never used protection but, before he could, Stephanie threw an ash tray at him! It missed Sha's head by inches.

"Steph, chill! Hold up-" he was able to say as she cried and began to throw everything she could get her hands on.

It was a wonder Shakim was able to get out of her house without injury. That was the angriest he ever saw Stephanie.

Sha smiled at the memory and was happy he was able to win back her confidence. Stephanie was his dawg.

A comedian using the moniker, Monkey, had the crowd in stitches as he snapped on any and everybody that caught his attention.

"Excuse me, main man . . . Yeah, you with that red and black checker board jacket! You play chess?"

The crowd was already screaming in laughter and so was the guy that Monkey was talking to, but the guy still managed to answer the question.

"Nah man, I don't play chess."

That was Monkey's cue.

"You could've fooled me, you up in here looking like a portable chess board!"

Monkey bent over and slapped his thigh.

"I was looking for the chess pieces, shit, I was ready to call next. Nah, nah, I'm just messing with you, I'm a comedian ya'll-- this is just comedy. But for real, is that your lady?" Monkey asked in a serious tone, pointing at the female who sat next to the guy in the checkered jacket.

Dude nodded his head up and down with a smile as he

looked over at his woman.

"Okay Big dawg, you got yourself a winner-- she's pretty," Monkey said and then continued, "Shawty looks like a pretty monster."

That joke there had people knocking things over and spitting out their drinks! Sha was holding his stomach he was laughing so hard! Everyone in the club knew that Monkey deserved to be on T.V.

In the middle of Monkey's performance, Sha felt his cell phone vibrating. He looked at the screen and saw that it was Sean Howard.

"Steph, I'll be right back-- it's Sean." Sha said before squeezing between tables and making his way to the bathroom.

"Sean, what's good?" Sha asked with a finger pressed in his ear to block out the show.

"Hey, Sha! I was just calling to tell you that I rescheduled the appointment we had to see that property on Hillside avenue that you're interested in. It's for tomorrow at 1:00, is that okay?"

"Yeah Sean, that's cool. Are we still meeting at Colossal realty?"

"That's correct."

"Okay, I'll let my uncle know and we'll see you tomorrow."

"Great. You have a good evening Sha."

"I sure will." Sha said before hanging up.

Shakim pulled out his pack of Newports and saw that he had two woolie blunts left from earlier. He debated lighting one up right there but decided there would be plenty of time later. As he lit up a cigarette, Shakim reflected on the habit he was developing with the crack filled blunts. He knew he needed to get it under control and quick.

'After these last two woos, that's it!' he resolved as he walked out of the bathroom.

As Sha attempted to squeeze through the tables on his way back to his seat, two things happened. One, the comedian Monkey had zeroed in on him. And two, a familiar face caught his attention. It was Steve, Steve was standing near the bar watching Sha like a hawk.

CHAPTER 13

Jeff and Rondu were at the back of the dorm smoking trees and blowing the smoke out the window. Rondu, being the true vet that he was, continuously squeezed baby powder into the palm of his hand before blowing it into the air to camouflage the smell.

Jeff was feeling a bit more confident after he took a long hot shower and changed into fresh clothes. Tasia had come through for him like he knew she would.

After they finished smoking, Rondu began to school Jeff on a few of the basics pertaining to how to do time.

"Son, next time somebody takes something of yours, fuck all of that talking shit—you gotta make an example! This is the terror dome, son, and it's only two types of individuals; Wolves and Prey. Niggaz gotta get in where they fit in!" Rondu was saying as if Jeff was his pupil.

They were standing next to Jeff's bed and Rondu picked up one of the shirts that Tasia had brought on the visit.

"Let me show you how this go," Rondu said lifting up Jeff's mattress, "fold all your shit up neatly and keep it under your mattress so your shit will stay semi presentable. We don't got no iron so niggaz gotta improvise, you feel me?"

"No doubt." Jeff said paying close attention.

"This is School of hard knocks 101. All your cosmetics; soap, toothpaste, deodorant and shit, all of that goes on top of the locker. The only thing that goes inside the locker is socks, drawers, tee shirts, and miscellaneous shit."

The other inmates inside the dorm sat around playing cards and talking quietly amongst themselves, but for the most part, everybody was aware that Rondu had taking a liking to Jeff and was schooling him to the game.

"Who came to see you?" Rondu asked as Jeff folded his clothes.

"My moms and my girl."

"Word? Was it crowded out there?"

"A little bit. And the visit was crazy short, it don't even feel like I was out there for a whole hour." Jeff complained.

"What police was out there?"

"I don't know his name, but, it was a skinny dude with dreads."

'Yes!' Rondu thought as Jeff described C.O. Taylor. Taylor was Rondu's homie from Jamaica, Queens, and he had been working the visiting room since Rondu's last tour of C-74. Rondu wasn't going to blow the spot up but Taylor was a street dude in a uniform, and as such he would bring in anything he was asked to bring in . . . for a small price.

"Don't even sweat that, son," Rondu said and then continued "let me make a few moves, word to my mother, they gonna think we live on the dance floor. Where your people coming from?"

"You know where American Towers is at?" Jeff asked.

"Son, I'm from Southside! Why wouldn't I know where American Towers is at? That's where you're from?"

"Yeah, yeah. I live right across the street."

"Okay, so you're right off of Merrick and Linden. My man Meek, God bless the dead, use to have American Towers on smash. You don't know fat Marvin, he's from the Towers?"

"Yeah I know Marvin! Marvin Fork, that's my dude"

"Word? Who was you fucking with out there, you was hustling, right?"

"Nah, I'm a working dude." Jeff said proudly and then continued, "I work at the vegetable market on 116th and Guy R. Brewer, right next to Baisley projects."

"The joint right next to the Long Island railroad overpass, I know where you're talking about. But damn, if you wasn't hustling, what the fuck they lock you up for?"

It seemed unusually quiet in the dorm as those in proximity awaited Jeff's response.

Jeff spoke humbly, in a soft tone, but those listening heard him loud and clear.

"Murder."

Later on when they called medication run, Rondu was back to running the hallways. He came up with a walkman for Jeff and another pillow case filled with cookies and potato chips.

Back in Mod six, a kid name Jazz from the Bronx was helping dudes write letters to their girls. Jeff was laughing to himself as he listened to the bullshit they composed.

"Take it from the top, Black, let, let, let me hear what you got so far," Jazz stuttered giving Jeff a knowing smile.

The big black gorilla looking guy named Black cleared

his throat before reading what he had written so far.

"Dear Crystal... By the time this documentation of conversation reaches it's destination, I hope it finds you in a deep state of meditation, so you can clearly understand my situation, which is my incarceration."

Jeff laid down on his bed and buried his head in his pillow so no one could see him cracking up laughing. He laughed until his stomach began to hurt, and just when he was able to regain some control, another guy named Young started reading the end of his letter.

"-Now I'm going to act like an artist and draw this letter to an end."

Jeff literally had tears in his eyes.

When Rondu came back to the dorm they smoked more trees and listened to Hot 97 on the radio.

"Ayo! I got somebody that will bring some smoke in on a regular basis. If you got somebody on the outside that will contribute to the cause we can do it real big." Rondu proposed.

"How much you need me to contribute?" Jeff asked. As long as he didn't have to take the risk he was with whatever.

"Whatever you want, but you have to give up an extra hundred dollars for every move so my people can live."

"That aint about nothing, let's do it." Jeff said.

Rondu explained how it was going down and Jeff gave Rondu Tasia's cell phone number so the connect could get in touch with her. All Jeff had to do was call his Boo and let her know to expect the phone call and handle business.

Jeff was making a smooth transition, but on Rikers Island a person needed to always beware of the unexpected... and Jeff was no exception.

CHAPTER 14

Tasia was preoccupied but determined to push forward. She arrived at the offices of Colossal Realty prepared to do whatever was necessary to get her back on track. Jeff's ordeal had caused her to call in sick for two consecutive days and Tasia couldn't afford to miss not even a day's pay.

"Hey Tasia!" Ebony said in a cheerful tone as Tasia entered the office accompanied by the sound of the chimes that hung above the entrance.

Ebony was Tasia's co-worker, a dark chocolate complex-ioned young lady who always seemed to be in high spirits. Her desk was right next to Tasia's cubicle.

"Good morning." Tasia responded politely as she made her way to her desk and hung her purse on a hook on the wall.

Colossal Realty was a boutique operation, it's small office was decorated with wall to wall carpet and four small desks with computers to accommodate the staff. Three metal fold up chairs served as a waiting area while a rectangular table on which a coffee machine and a microwave co-existed qualified as the official break area and lounge. There was a bathroom and a utility closet to the left at the back of the premises, and to the right was a huge office that belonged to the CEO; Keith Armstrong.

"Is Mr. Charlie here yet?" Tasia asked as she sat down and turned on her computer.

The staff at Colossal referred to Keith Armstrong as Mr. Charlie because he often adopted the demeanor of a slave master. They often complained that he ran the office like a plantation.

"Yep!" Ebony said in a conspiratorial tone, rolling her chair closer to Tasia, "And he was good and mad about you missing that appointment with Sean Howard. He said you should've been closed that deal, and Linda with her trifling self had the nerve to agree with him. She was talking about: 'Tasia didn't close that deal yet?" Mr. Armstrong said if you don't secure that deal by today he's going to do it himself.

Tasia rolled her eyes. She knew good and well Mr. Armstrong wasn't going to take that project away from her. If Mr. Armstrong was Mrs. Armstrong, Tasia pondered with a smirk, it might've been a problem. But Mr. Armstrong, like most men Tasia encountered had a weakness for a woman's flesh. From day one when Mr. Armstrong first saw Tasia, she knew from that look in his eyes that he was a slave of his own desires.

"He's just talking to hear himself talk," Tasia said as she furiously tapped on the keys of her computer.

Ebony giggled. It was common knowledge that Tasia had the boss wrapped around her little finger.

As Tasia examined the file for the Hillside avenue property her mind drifted to Jeff. Her baby was wrongly accused for murder and trapped on Rikers Island.

Tasia had a deep respect for Jeff, it was almost as if she worshipped the ground he walked on. Unlike the majority of the male species, Jeff didn't wear his lust and desires as a badge of honor. He had wants and desires like everyone else, but, Jeff's self control was amazing... he simply wouldn't allow his lusts to control him.

Tasia thought back to the days when they first started dating, back when she thought Jeff was still a virgin. Jeff use to act as if he was scared of the pussy! There was the time when Tasia grabbed him by the hand and led him to her bedroom. Up until that point they had only gone to the movies together and occasionally Jeff had splurged on dinner at a nice restaurant. When they got to Tasia's room she was hot and she wanted Jeff to make a move, even if they didn't have sex she wanted to play! It was as if Jeff didn't have a clue, he was being a gentleman as he patiently looked around her room at the posters of Usher and other R&B acts hanging on her wall. Then, obviously uninterested in getting intimate, Jeff occupied himself with Tasia's extensive selection of CD's and DVD's.

Tasia was hot and bothered, but she wasn't giving up that easy. "Damn Tay," Jeff said as Tasia disappeared into her closet, "What you know about Alexander O'neil? I see you got the 'Hearsay' CD."

"I love that CD," Tasia yelled from inside the closet, "Go ahead and put it on."

Jeff nodded his head in agreement as he fumbled around with Tasia's CD player before figuring out how to work it. He had his favorite song playing softly when Tasia finally came out of the closet.

'She touched me with, a heart of gold, I can't go one day with out my sunshine...'

Tasia turned the heat up donning some pink boy shorts that couldn't conceal her derriere, and a cut off pink t-shirt that exposed her entire mid section allowing her to showoff her belly ring.

Jeff merely glanced in her direction, "Ayo!" he said shaking his head from side to side, "This is my mutha fucking song!"

And then, as if Tasia didn't exist, Jeff sat on a wicker chair by the window, closed his eyes and enjoyed the music.

Tasia paraded around the room scantily dressed pretending to be busy until Jeff finally opened his eyes. He was watching her closely and Tasia thought he had finally came around, until he said, "Girl, find somewhere and sit your ass down! And put some clothes on, don't you have any respect for yourself?"

Tasia just stood there with her mouth open. She couldn't believe she just got played like that. Everywhere she went men always desired her-- even at, or especially at, church. Although she was heated and slightly embarrassed, Tasia knew right then and there that Jeff was different. He was, in fact, special.

Inwardly Tasia smiled at the memory, and then she flashed back to the conversation she had with Jeff just the previous night when he was finally able to call again. Jeff had said something about someone calling her, and he wanted her to give the person three hundred dollars. Tasia didn't know what that was all about but she had Jeff's back 100%, and if Jeff wanted her to give someone three hundred dollars, then it was good as done.

The chimes above the door sounded throughout the office as another real estate agent, Linda, came strutting inside dressed in the latest fashion and walking as if she was on a runway.

"Good morning," Linda sang to no one in particular.

Tasia looked up and shot a disgusted look in Linda's direction before continuing to tap away at her key board.

"Hey Linda," Ebony said in her usual cheerful demeanor.

Linda poured herself a cup of coffee and then made her way to her desk which was right behind Tasia's cubicle.

"Mr. Charlie here yet?" Linda asked after catching eye contact with Ebony.

Ebony stole a glance toward Mr. Armstrong's office before nodding her head up and down, smiling the whole time.

Linda blew steam away from her coffee before taking a sip, "I see Tasia is back, thank God." she said before addressing Tasia directly, "Girl, Mr. Armstrong be acting like he can't function when you're not here. I had to set his ass straight, he was tripping about that Hillside avenue property not being sold-- I thought you been closed that deal Tasia?"

Tasia stopped what she was doing and spun her chair around to face Linda, "Why are you all up in my business? Do you need for me to find something for you to do?" Tasia's words dripped with venom as she blasted Linda, "I'm only going to tell you this once, when I'm not here-- stay the fuck out of my business! Don't worry about whether or not I closed a deal, worry about yourself! That's why your ass is always in the middle of some bullshit-- learn how to mind your business."

At the sound of Tasia raising her voice Mr. Armstrong appeared and stood in the doorway of his office. He looked around smoothly trying to access the situation, but, Tasia just as quickly turned back to her computer, and Ebony and Linda busied themselves with something or another.

"Is everything alright out here?" he asked in a tone of amusement.

94

The ladies agreed that it was and Mr. Armstrong let out a chuckle, "Tasia, when you get a minute I need to see you in my office . . . and Ebony, do me a favor and bring me a cup of coffee will ya".

Ebony hurriedly granted Mr. Armstrong's request and fetched him some coffee. While Ebony was leaving the CEO's office Tasia was on her way in.

Mr. Armstrong sat behind his massive desk with his tie loosened and his sleeves rolled up. The forty-six year old had the build of a NFL linebacker. The diamond cut wedding band on his left hand told the story of a wife at home, yet Mr. Armstrong sat behind his desk undressing Tasia with his eyes as if the vows he once uttered were merely a formality.

"Please, close the door behind you." Mr. Armstrong insisted, immediately feeling a rush of blood in his groin area.

Tasia was in no mood for her supervisor's not so subtle advances but she did as she was told because she enjoyed her job. Instead of exposing her feelings she smiled and turned on the charm.

"Don't be mad at me Mr. Armstrong, there's no excuse why I haven't closed that deal with Sean Howard. It's just that-"

"Whoa, baby girl, you wait one minute." Mr. Armstrong interjected smoothly as he stood up and came around the desk.

Tasia noticed with disdain when he momentarily groped himself under the guise of adjusting his crotch, and she almost recoiled when he placed his perverted hands on her shoulders and gently began to give her a deep tissue massage.

"When you called me and said you had a family emergency I didn't ask no questions. I trust you Tasia, you don't need to explain nothing." he said as he allowed his hands to slide a little to her tender arms, "you take as much time as you need with that deal. With the economy the way it is I can't expect you to close a deal everyday, and let me say this, you've been doing an excellent job from the first day I hired you, and I mean that. Now, is everything okay with the family? You don't need any additional days off do you, because it's hell when you're not here but, for you babygirl I can sure 'nuff make it happen..."

"No, everything is fine now, thank you." Tasia said as she stood there with Mr. Armstrong looking deeply into her eyes.

"Are you sure?"

Tasia nodded her head up and down and said, "Yes Keith"

Mr. Armstrong loved when they were alone and she called him by his first name. His dick got harder than King Kong's knuckles.

"Come here and give me a hug!" He said embracing Tasia and inhaling deeply, "Damn baby girl, you're smelling like strawberries and cream up in here. When are you going to stop playing and let Keith take you out?"

Tasia smiled as she noticed the hint of desperation in his voice. Mr. Armstrong was pathetic.

"As soon as you get tired of your wife and get a divorce."

"I'll leave her in a heartbeat!" Mr. Armstrong shot back.

"What about your kids?"

"Shit, I'll leave them too!" he said only half joking.

Tasia quickly put things in their right perspective, "That's why I enjoy working for you so much Mr. Armstrong, you have a good sense of humor and you're down to earth. If I thought you was serious about leaving your wife and kids I don't know if I would be able to respect you."

Tasia smiled and Mr. Armstrong sighed.

"Okay, you win again. But one of these days Tasia, one of these days . . ."

Tasia winked at him seductively and strutted out of his office.

'Damn!' Mr. Armstrong thought as he fondled himself, *'baby girl is finer than a mother fucker!'*

CHAPTER 15

"You looking for my mommy?" the little boy asked swinging the door open wide enough for Shakim to enter.

"Yeah little man, I'm looking for your mommy, but I'm also looking for you. What's happening, are you alright?" Shakim asked as he surveyed the living room.

There were clothes everywhere! Big green garbage bags filled with dirty looking clothes were on the couch, next to the couch, behind the couch, and then there were some clothes just scattered across the floor. Sha had to watch his step because he almost stepped on a shitty pamper that was being bum rushed by flies. That accounted for the foul smell.

"I'm okay, I was just eating breakfast." little man said as he ran back to the table to reclaim a bowl of cereal that a black cat had its face in. "Leave my food alone, Tiger!" he said, picking the cat up and tossing him onto a bag of clothes.

'This shit is crazy!' Sha thought before asking the little boy where his mother was at.

"She sleep!" he said pointing toward the back of the house.

Sha navigated his way down a cluttered hallway and stopped in the doorway of the bedroom where Shelly was sprawled across her bed with her mouth open snoring loudly.

Sha picked up a dirty sock and threw it over Shelly's face.

"What the fuck? Buddy, Imma beat your ass—" Shelly yelled looking around crazy.

Shakim was standing there smiling, he couldn't believe this bad bitch could be so nasty.

"Good morning stinky breath." he said venturing farther into the room.

"Sha? What the hell you doing here? I thought you was my crazy ass son, I was gonna whoop that ass!"

"The question is: what the fuck are you doing in bed at 10 o'clock in the morning? I could've been coming to take you shopping or something and you in here sounding like a lawn mower."

Sha sat at the edge of the bed.

"I do not snore with your lying ass, and I damn sure know you wasn't trying to take a bitch shopping. Nine times out of ten you just came to get some pussy." Shelly said reaching over to play with the zipper on Sha's pants.

Shakim thought of the possibility of Shelly being the one that burned him and that reminded him about the mission he was on.

"Nah," he said reaching in his pocket and pulling out some weed. "I aint thinking about no pussy. I got an appointment at 1:00, I told you I'm trying to cop this new building. I just came to blow some weed with you before I go-- if that's cool with you."

"You know I'm down Sha, that's why you came over. You don't got nothing to put in it?" Shelly asked slyly.

Sha pulled out a folded up hundred dollar bill, "You think I don't?" he asked as he used a nickel to crush the crack up into a powdery substance.

He proceeded to gut a blunt before refilling it with weed lacing it up with a generous amount of crack. Shelly jumped up and quickly cleared the doorway so she could close the door. When she turned back around, Sha was on the bed with his dick out.

"I don't got time for no serious fucking, but, let a nigga get a little head before we hit this."

Raheem was standing in front of his house when Sha pulled up in the Range.

"If we're late I'm cutting you off--true story!" Raheem said sliding in the passenger seat.

"It's only 12:30 Unc, we aint gonna be late." Sha said as he pulled off.

"What time were you suppose to pick me up?" Raheem asked leaning over and sniffing the air, "Ayo! What was you doing, smoking crack?"

That shit caught Sha off guard, but, the youngster was a quick thinker.

"Crack? You tripping Unc, what you saying-- I smell like crack?" Sha asked sniffing his clothes.

"That's exactly what I'm saying!" Raheem spit with a look in his eyes that Sha never witnessed before.

"Oh!" Sha said banging his hand against the steering wheel, "I know what that is . . . last night I took Stephanie to Manhattan Proper, and I didn't wanna tell you but I've been having problems with a few cats from around the way, so I went to check my man Boogie to get some heat. Boogie runs a crack spot, and I went to drop the joint back off a little while ago they were up in their smoking that shit. For a minute there I thought you was tripping."

Raheem looked at his nephew skeptically but he was somewhat relieved that there was an explanation. The last thing he wanted was for Shakim to end up like his mother.

"Who have you been having problems with?" Raheem pressed.

Sha took a deep breath and exhaled slowly, "Mainly it's this older cat name Steve."

"Steve?" Raheem asked, "What Steve, where's he from?"

"I think he's from Forty, he be with Kaymel and the dude Green-eyes that just got killed.

"You're talking about Steve O, I know exactly who you're talk about." Raheem said nodding his head as he contemplated, "Let me take care of that, meanwhile, keep your ass out of crack-houses and stay the fuck away from guns."

When they pulled up in front of Colossal Realty it was five minutes before one. Raheem spotted Sean Howard's red M5 BMW but Sean was nowhere to be found. Raheem pulled out his cell phone and called him to let him know they were out front.

When Sean Howard came out with Tasia, Shakim just about lost his mind.

"Got damn!" he yelled like he didn't have any sense.

Raheem turned around to see what happened and then looked back at his nephew with disgust. Raheem just shook his head.

"I think we're going to get a blood test done because we can't be related." he said in defeat.

"I'm sorry Unc, but damn! That bi-, I mean, babygirl is gorgeous. Raheem ignored him and stepped out of the whip.

"Glad you could make it Raheem, this is Ms. Brown."

"Hello," Raheem said stolidly, although Tasia's beauty hadn't escaped him.

"Do you mind if we ride with you? It would make more sense with gas prices being the way they are." Sean suggested.

Raheem thought about his crazy ass nephew, "No, I'm sure Sha won't mind." he said as they piled into the Range Rover.

As they pulled off, Raheem couldn't help but to think it was going to be a long day.

CHAPTER 16

"Ayo! Put some water on that shit!" someone yelled from the shower area.

In mod six the showers were right next to the toilet stalls. Jeff reached behind him and gave a courtesy flush. His stomach was bubbling like crazy and it felt like he was pissing out of his ass.

"That's you in there Jeff?" Rondu's voice boomed through the stall.

"Yeah," Jeff responded mortified.

"You good at math?" Rondu asked.

'They got me in a fucking nut house!' Jeff thought. "Yeah, why? What's up?" Jeff asked getting frustrated.

"You need to ADD some water to that shit, that's why! That's what the fuck is up!" Rondu roared getting a good laugh out of those in the vicinity.

When Jeff finally came out of the bathroom for the third time a kid named Big House from the Bronx was sitting on the bed next to his putting on deodorant and lotioning up. It was obvious that Big House was just getting out of the shower but Jeff couldn't understand why dude was gritting on him.

Jeff didn't know what dude's problem was and he really didn't care for-real because his motto was the same, *'As long as a nigga don't put his hands on me...'*

One of the bloods from sound view projects in the BX peeped Big House looking vexed and made his way over to see what was popping.

"Big House, fuck you over here with your face frowned up for?"

"Man Nut, don't come over here with all that playing shit. I'm ready to break this bird ass nigga up!" Big House said nodding in Jeff's direction.

"What happened?" Nut asked, his voice filled with fake concern.

"Nah, first this nigga kept me up half the night with his snoring, then I go to take a shower and this nigga got the whole bathroom smelling like hot crackhead pussy on a summer day. I'm tight right now that's my word!" Big House said as he slipped into a pair of green sweat pants and then began tying up his sneakers.

"I aint gonna front, yo'!" Nut said putting gas on the fire, "he had it smelling like a nigga shitted on the floor or something. We smelled it all the way in here."

Jeff was fighting to control his tongue, he couldn't believe these dudes were tripping over him taking a dump.

"Yeah," Big House said taking Jeff's silence as weakness, "he got one more time to cross my path and I'm smashing him."

"Nigga you aint smashing shit," Jeff said without raising his voice. He'd had enough of the buffoonery. "Yall niggaz got me twisted!"

Jeff's open challenge surprised the shit out of everybody in proximity. It wasn't just what he said as much as the way he said it. Nevertheless, he threw Big House for a loop.

"Oh shit!" Nut yelled amping it up, "It's about to go

down!"

By then Big House had regained his composure, "What? You bitch ass nigga, I will crush you! You trying to see me?"

Big House was making a scene and dudes started posting up around the dorm waiting to see what was going to happen. Rondu was in the T.V. room, but he was a cold vet, he could tell by the way niggaz was acting that something was going down.

"Nigga you faking," Jeff was telling House in that same monotone when Rondu came in the dorm area.

Big House moved quick throwing a two piece that Jeff easily deflected.

"Hold up! Hold the fuck up!" Rondu yelled and then continued, "Yall niggaz take that shit to the back. Ayo Jazz, watch out for the c.o."

The kid Jazz strategically positioned himself where he could keep an eye out for five-O, and it was fight night like Las Vegas in Mod six.

"Yeah nigga come on!" Big House said rushing in throwing powerful blows.

Jeff was playing defense but one of House's blows caught him on the side of the head and it felt like someone hit him with a rock in a sock!

"That's all you got big boy?" Jeff asked dancing out of the way.

A heckler with front row seats said, "He almost knocked your fucking head off!"

Big House charged in again, this time Jeff dipped to his left and came up throwing a flurry of punches. Big House staggered and fell up against the wall but instead of Jeff finishing him off he just danced around a little bit as if he was just getting warm.

Niggaz in the dorm were going crazy! Nobody would've thought that Jeff was nice with his hands.

Big House tried to shake it off and regain his composure, but now he was being cautious. No more charging.

"What's up Big House," Jeff asked tauntingly as they danced around as if they were in a ring, "You didn't get enough yet?"

Jeff would fake like he was about to swing and Big House would cover up like a storm was coming.

Jeff was smiling now, "You had all that mouth, you ready big boy? I'm about to put you on your ass, you ready?"

House wasn't saying nothing! Jeff faked again and when House covered up Jeff punished his mid section with body blows. House dropped his hands and exposed his face, after that it only took one punch. Jeff shot from the shoulder and tapped that jaw! Big House was sleep on his feet before he crumbled to the floor. Jeff raised both hands in the air as a sign of victory and the dorm was going bananas!

They ended up taking House to the hospital for a broken jaw. His shit had to get wired up and he was forced to adhere to a liquid diet for the months that followed.

Still, Jeff remained humble. Later that night after the fight he called Tasia. She was in a good mood because she closed the deal with Shakim. Her commission was only one percent but she made $6,000 off of that deal.

"I'm proud of you, you know that right?"

"Awwwww, thank you! I spoke to the lawyer too, I finally convinced him to take your case." Tasia said excitedly.

"Word? How much is he charging?" Jeff asked knowing

that money would be tight.

"Don't worry about that Boo, I got this. He's gonna try to get you a bail hearing too, he said he can't make no promises but he's going to see what he can do."

"That's what's up, babygirl. I love you, ya heard?"

"Yeah. I love you too, Jeff!"

Rondu was flagging Jeff trying to get him to ask Tasia about the money.

"Oh yeah, did them people ever get in touch with you about that three hundred dollars?"

"Yeah, I spoke to the guy about an hour ago. He's supposed to be on his way over."

That was good news! Jeff spoke to Tasia a little while longer before letting someone else use the phone. Then he jetted to the bathroom because his stomach was bubbling again.

When Tasia got off the phone with Jeff, she flipped through the channels trying to find something to watch on T.V. When nothing caught her attention she decided to read some of the book she recently purchased, 'Only God Can Judge Me: The Life and times of Tyran "Tah-Tah" Moore.

Tah-Tah was from around her way. When Tasia was younger she remembered he used to have the smoke gray M3 BMW. She used to have a crush on Tah-Tah.

Tasia read the book as if it were a gossip tabloid. She didn't know that Tah-Tah was the one who took Nas' QB medallion! And then he had the nerve to sell it back to him? Tasia couldn't believe that. And why on earth would they think that Tah-Tah killed Jam Master Jay, especial 1) if he was all the way in Los Angelas when it happened?

People are always spreading rumors Tasia thought as she put the book down and went to answer her door. When Tasia opened the door she was in for a surprise. The guy standing at her door that she was suppose to give money to for Jeff was the same C.O. from the visiting room on Rikers Island; the one with the dreadlocks and gold teeth. Tasia stood there with her mouth open as officer Taylor undressed her with his eyes.

"Damn, I knew you looked familiar!"

CHAPTER 17

The music blared from huge speakers. Grand Master Vic was playing one of his favorite songs of all time, Rising To The Top, which became the Southside national anthem in the 1980's,

'Give it all you got, give-it all you got'

(The crowd screaming) "keep rising to the top,"

They were behind P.S.40 in the school's large playground known in Jamaica Queens as 40 park, and they were having a block party in honor of the late Green Eyes.

The young and the old, male and female, paper chasers and broke ass individuals all came together to celebrate the memory of thus another fallen soldier. Most of the people in attendance wore T-shirts that displayed a picture of Green Eyes in his prime, his platinum jewelry with diamonds nearly as radiant as his youthful smile. The black Cadillac Escalade that Green Eyes was often seen driving through the hood was parked in the middle of the school yard. Steve, Kaymel, and a bunch of Green Eyes' nieces and nephews were sitting atop the truck watching the festivities. Guys were racing Gixxers up and down 160th Street while a few riders actually came into the park and were doing all types of tricks, from indos to doughnuts.

Young boys with dreams of being the next Lebron James were running full court basketball games while the young girls jumped double-dutch or tried to outdo each other doing the latest dances.

The older crowd were relaxing on the benches and beach chairs drinking beer, playing spades, and more less enjoying the moment.

Barbeque grills were smoking as hamburgers, hotdogs, chicken and steaks were grilled to perfection and served to all whom had an appetite to eat.

Little Gabe was strapped as usual and he just stood leaning against the Cadillac Escalade watching the vicinity with a careful eye. This being the case, it was no wonder that Gabe was the first to notice Shakim's black Range Rover as it slowed down and double parked across the street from the school yard. Gabe tapped Steve's leg to put him on point but Steve was already on it.

"Imma get this nigga," Gabe said as a matter of fact.

"Be easy!" Steve suggested as he watched Shakim and a bald head dude jumping out of the Range.

"Who's that, son?" Kaymel asked.

"That's the little nigga Sha that I was telling you about, he used to hustle in Baisley. Faggot ass nigga came up on some cheese somehow, me and Gabe is just waiting for the opportunity to snatch his little ass up." Steve said.

Shakim was stunting! He wore a black tee that accentuated his platinum chain with the iced out Mickey Mouse medallion swinging from his neck. For insurance he also had a chrome 40 cal tucked in his waist and an extra clip in his back pocket.

The bald head dude with him had a golden brown complexion, and an athletic build. He wore a New York knick jersey that exposed thick arms that were cut up like a bad bag of dope, and ole boy had a swagger that exuded smooth confidence.

As they strolled into the park the bald head guy studied the surroundings until he spotted Steve sitting atop the Escalade. Him and Shakim began walking in that direction.

Grand Master Vic was playing the 50 Cents song 'I Get Money', and everybody was either doing the wop or dancing while they shook their hand in the air as if they were rolling dice.

Steve jumped down off of the truck and Kaymel warned him," Don't start no shit up in here, this is for Green Eyes."

It wasn't until Shakim and the bald head dude were within thirty feet of the truck that Steve recognized the bald head dude's face.

"Oh shit! Get the fuck outta here," Steve yelled in amazement. "That's Raheem! That's my mutha fuckin' man!"

Raheem smiled as Steve embraced him with a big ass hug, but Gabe was off to the side watching Shakim skeptically.

"I heard you was home. Niggaz been saying you was home but you know how that go, I don't believe nothing I hear and only half the shit I see. . . Damn, what you been up to?" Steve asked.

Raheem was a smooth dude for real. He peeped Gabe's demeanor and knew the young boy was strapped, and he also knew that Steve was uncomfortable not knowing how Shakim fit into what appeared to be a planned reunion.

"You already know, Steve, you can find me involved in anything that's paying the bills. Never the less, my biggest challenge right now is trying to keep this little knuckle head out of trouble," Raheem said nodding toward Shakim, " I swear, if he wasn't my nephew --"

"That's your nephew?" Steve asked surprised, glancing

at Sha and then back to Raheem.

"Unfortunately." Raheem responded with a smile.

"That's my word I didn't know he was your nephew. And I already know you gotta know I was scheming on son, that's what brought you back to the hood, so something good did come out of this. I'm just glad shit didn't get out of hand. It wasn't nothing personal, Sha, ya heard?" Steve said and stuck his hand out.

Shakim accepted the truce and shook Steve's hand.

"Gabe, that shit is dead, for now on this nigga is just like family." Steve declared.

Gabe had a smile ready and he came over and gave Sha some dap. "Raheem, don't you have a sister name Beverly?" Kaymel asked from the roof of the Escalade.

Raheem's head snapped up and he was looking at Kaymel but he didn't recognize the face, "Where you know my sister from?"

"Nah, my pops use to mess with Bev when I was little. I remember when you use to have the grey 560 Benz." Kaymel said respectfully.

"What's your pop's name?"

"Tim . . . Tim Bartee."

"Oh yeah?" Raheem said smiling at Kaymel, " Tim Bartee is your father? Tim is a good dude. Tell him I said to stop by my mom's house in St. Albans, he know where it's at. You remember Bev after all that time, huh?"

"Yeah, yeah, Bev was crazy cool. She use to spoil me."

Raheem's mood switched gears and he became somber as he thought about Beverly's addiction.

"Well, Bev aint too cool right now. Baby sis is caught up

in the streets. But that just goes to show you that the game will never let you go without paying a price, either you lose yourself, your freedom, or your soul -- either way it aint worth it."

"I know that's right." Kaymel agreed.

"That's her son right there," Raheem said pointing at Shakim.

"Word?" Kaymel said nodding as he stored Sha's face in his memory, "Well you don't have to worry about keeping him out of trouble. As long as he's in Jamaica Queens, he's straight. That's my word. Yall hungry? Come on, let's get something to eat!"

The rest of the day was peaceful in the projects. Grand Master Vic played some old Corey D tapes that had the older crowd singing along to Corey D's dedication rhyme. He played some old Rat and Monkey joints, Dada Rock, and he even mixed Rising to the top again while one of his boys did an old coke adds life routine.

This was the way Green Eyes would've wanted to be remembered, so Grand Master Vic did the best he could to send the fallen soldier out in style.

Before everybody departed, Steve gave Kaymel the latest developements of his investigation.

"Ayo! I spoke to Green Eyes' mother before she left. She told me they're having a bail hearing next Thursday for scrams that killed Green Eyes. I already told Doonie and Blast that we up in there, so you can chill if you want -- it's up to you."

"Nah son," Kaymel said with murder in his eyes, "count me in. If it's the last thing I do, I wanna see the face of the person who killed my little man. That way, even if I die, Imma catch that nigga in hell!"

CHAPTER 18

"What's the deal, Jawbreaker!" Rondu greeted Jeff.

Jeff was in the dayroom watching videos on BET. He was feeling aggravated because of his bouts with diarrhea, and he was also experiencing hot and cold chills which had interfered with his sleep the night before.

"You're a funny dude," he responded as he reached out and gave Rondu some dap.

"Smell this," Rondu said holding a sandwich bag of exotic weed under Jeff's nose, "Your girl came through with that loot. Come on let's go break this shit down."

Rondu spun around to leave the dayroom without checking to see if Jeff was following. As Rondu headed toward the back of the dorm he told a kid named Tiny to watch out for the C.O.

Jeff and Rondu set up shop on a vacant bunk and Rondu poured the contents of the sandwich bag onto a legal writing pad. He expertly used his jail identification card to break the weed down into thirds.

"You take one and I take one," Rondu said pointing at the separated piles, "we can use the rest to stack up on commissary. Pin joints go for $5 apiece."

And that's how it went, Jeff and Rondu put smoke in the

air and even let a few dudes live. Those that couldn't catch a free ride came up with soap, lotion, cigarettes, and anything with value so they could pay the going rate.

The atmosphere in the dorm was peaceful as everyone found their comfort zone, most of the guys had their headphones on jamming with their favorite radio station. When they played a Nas throwback, *It aint hard to tell*, dudes got excited and was singing along with the song.

'Deep like the shining, sparkle like a diamond, sneak a uzi on the Island in my army jacket lining...'

This was the way many inmates escaped the reality of being confined. They watched television, they played cards and board games for hours at a time, they did push-ups, they gambled, they got high, and they traded war stories. Inmates who could sing or rap fearlessly showcased their talents. Comedians played the dozen and told regurgitated jokes.

Half of the guys in the dorm were higher than a satellite and everyone was having a good time, and then a C.O. came and put a damper on the party.

"Okay, listen up! If I call your name, pack your property because you're going to population."

The C.O. proceeded to call ten names, both Jeff and Rondu were among those called. The mood in the dorm did a complete 360! Whereas guys were dancing around singing a moment ago, now everyone wore somber expressions.

"Let me see what the fuck is going on," Rondu said after a moment of silence.

The truth was, the guys in Mod six had become comfortable with one another. Sure, there were quarrels, but for the most part everyone knew what to expect. Now, Jeff was once again being thrust into the unknown.

When Rondu came back into the dorm Jeff could tell by the expression on his face that he didn't have good news. "Let me holler at you for a minute Jeff," he said leading the way to Jeff's bunk.

Rondu plopped down on the bed and Jeff sat next to him.

"They got you going to 4 upper. I tried to make moves and get you pulled to Mod eight with me but your classification level is too high--"

"My classification?" Jeff asked not understanding.

"Yeah, your security classification. Because of your case, they classified you high security, but don't worry, Queens niggaz are deep in 4 upper. Tell Freeze you're my mutha fuckin' people, and here, take this,"

Rondu opened up a match book and passed it to Jeff. There was a gem star razor blade neatly tucked behind the match sticks.

"What's this for?" Jeff asked, still green to the ways of his new reality.

Rondu sucked his teeth and took a deep breath, "Listen son, you aint no sucker ass nigga, that's why I fuck with you. You're a good dude, but sometimes good dudes have to learn how to be not so good in order to survive in hostile environments. If you go to 4 upper on some passive shit, them niggaz are gonna eat you alive. Listen to me Jeff! The first nigga that comes at you sideways like shit is sweet, you have to make an example out of him. Rep ya hood nigga, south-side don't raise no suckers. Once niggaz see you aint no sucker, then they're gonna respect you. If you wanna be a good dude after that, be my guest, but, from the door you gotta go super hard!"

Jeff digested everything Rondu was telling him. Afterwards, he mimicked the other guys who were leaving by packing all of his belongings onto a blanket he spread out on the floor. After tying the blanket at the four corners, Jeff dragged his stuff to the front door. As he stood up front and kicked it with Rondu while they waited to leave, a thought occurred to him.

"Ayo! Where am I going to hide the razor at?"

Rondu looked at him with a straight face and said, "Between your butt cheeks,"

Jeff looked at him all crazy to see if he was serious.

Rondu didn't crack a smile, and he was through talking!

CHAPTER 19

Tasia was in the middle of cleaning up around the house when she was interrupted by the ringing of the doorbell. She grabbed the trash out of the kitchen on her way to the door and got on her tip toes to peep out the window before she opened it up.

"Hey Missy!" Tasia said as she flung the trash bag over the fence with the rest of the garbage waiting to be picked up.

"Don't hey me!" Missy said as she waved to the guy in the Dodge Magnum that just dropped her off. She was letting the guy know he could leave, and he dutifully tapped the horn twice and disappeared into the night.

"Who was that?" Tasia asked leading the way inside the house.

"That was none of your damn business, I met him at the club the other night. But I'm asking the questions around here-- where have you been? And why haven't you been answering your phone or returning your messages?" Missy asked as they made their way into the living room, then continued in rapid succession, "And why didn't you tell me that Jeff is in jail? What happened?"

Tasia was cool with Missy's nosey butt asking a million questions, but the last two questions had her automatically heated.

"Who told you that Jeff is in jail?" she asked with attitude.

Missy got comfortable in the huge leather recliner facing the 55 gallon fish tank, "Girl calm down, when I couldn't catch up with you, I called your mother. She said that she spoke to you and that you was just coming back from Rikers Island. She said Jeff killed somebody. I told her that she must have got the story mixed up because I know good and well that Jeff didn't kill nobody."

Tasia sucked her teeth. She knew she couldn't trust her mother to keep her big mouth shut.

"You know what I'm thinking, right?" Tasia asked as she sprayed windex on the fish tank and began to clean the glass.

"No, what?" Missy asked.

"You can't tell a bitch nothing if you don't want everybody else to know."

That put Missy on the defensive, "Well excuse me, I didn't know it was a big secret. But you right, that aint none of my damn business--"

"Missy shut up. I'm talking about my mother, she's always putting my business on Broadway and I specifically asked her not to tell anybody. You know you're my girl and I was going to let you know what's going on but it wasn't her business to tell you, just like it's not your business to tell anybody else." Tasia said with authority.

"Well, you don't have to worry about me telling nobody. Do Ronnie know?"

Veronica, aka Ronnie was the third member of their crew, together they were like three the hard way.

"Girl, I haven't even spoken to Ronnie yet. I've been so

119

busy trying to keep everything in order it's hard to find time to think." Tasia complained, then without warning she broke down and started crying.

"Missy, they got him for murder! They caught him at the scene of the crime and he was carrying the gun that killed the guy."

Missy got up and rushed over to her girl, hugging her and offering support.

"It's okay, girl. It has to be a reasonable explanation because we both know Jeff aint no killer."

"The lawyer thinks it's an open and shut case, he didn't even want to represent Jeff!"

Missy was rocking Tasia and patting her on the back. At the same time she was digesting everything she was being told. On the low, Missy was to some degree jealous of Tasia's relationship with Jeff. Her jealousy never reached the level of being diabolical but at the same time it definitely wasn't all good. Missy secretly wondered why she couldn't be the one in a meaningful relationship. Why she had to be the one that ended up with men that only wanted one thing. Missy harbored these feelings, but, at the end of the day she would never have wished this ordeal on Tasia.

Missy and Tasia sat down and talked for over an hour before Missy asked Tasia to call her a cab.

"Girl stop tripping," Tasia said getting up and grabbing her car keys, "I'll drop you off, I need to get some air anyway."

After Tasia dropped Missy off in front of her building on 88th Avenue, she drove to the Dunkin Donuts by her job on Hillside Ave. After treating herself to an assortment of fresh donuts she made her way back to her car with the newly acquired cache of goodies. She pulled into traffic and didn't make it a block away when a gust of smoke began to rise from the hood of her car. Sucking her teeth, Tasia quickly pulled over to the side of the road and turned the car off. Turning on the hazard lights she looked in the side view mirror before stepping out to see what the problem was. When Tasia lifted the hood, a cloud of smoke raced to the sky. Tasia wanted to cry!

"When it rains it pours!" she said fanning the smoke and taking two steps back.

As Tasia stood there contemplating her next move, a black 645 BMW crept up beside her, Freddy Jackson's *'Rock Me Tonight'* could be heard emerging from its speakers.

'Hey girl, long time no see . . . do you have a little time to spend with me --'

Tasia glanced into the vehicle and the familiar face in the driver' seat was a welcomed intruder. It was James Carter, the practical joker.

"You look like you can use a hand," James said hoping he could be of assistance. Remembering the way their last encounter went, he waited for Tasia to give him the green light as opposed to lust jumping out and imposing on the comely damsel in distress.

"Yes, I can definitely use some help." Tasia admitted, giving James Carter a perfunctory smile.

"Well let me see what I can do," James said hopping out of the coupe and coming around to take a look under her hood.

"It looks like your radiator is busted," he said after a minute, "but don't get me to lying. I get paid for moving cars off the lot and I let the mechanics get paid for making sure everything is straight under the hood. A friend of mine owns a tow truck company, he owes me a favor so I'll just have him tow your car to my lot and I'll have my mechanics take a look under the hood in the morning. Meanwhile I can give you a lift home if you'll let me do the honor."

Tasia was irresolute but it was really a no brainer.

"Let me get my stuff from out of the car. And you better give me a bill for all of this, the least I can do is pay the bill." Tasia said knowing that nothing in life was free.

James Carter just smiled as he closed the hood of her car. He hated to prey on a beautiful woman at a vulnerable moment, but, he wouldn't have missed this opportunity for nothing in the world.

As Tasia got her belongings and slid into the passenger seat of the coupe, R. Kelly's *'Seems Like You're Ready'* was playing softly in the background.

'Temperatures rising . . . your body's yearning'

"So," James Carter said as he pulled into traffic, "you never did tell me your name."

CHAPTER 20

4 upper, like all of the other dorms and cell blocks in
C-74, consisted of two sides; a Northside and a Southside.
However, the cell-blocks in C-74 were considerably smaller than
the dormitories. Whereas dormitories such as Mod six had the
capacity to hold up to a hundred inmates with fifty beds being on
each side, the cellblocks such as 4 upper only had the capacity to
hold up to sixty inmates, there were thirty cells on each side.

Jeff was standing in the vestibule of 4 upper where he
was met by an officer whom shared a strong resemblance with
the actor that played Mr. T on the television series 'The A Team'.
The officer wore an abundance of thick gold chains, he had big
gold rings on almost every finger of both hands, and his muscles
were seemingly bursting out from everywhere as he sized Jeff
up with a menacing scowl.

Jeff had a little knuckle game but he only weighed a buck
eighty with all of his clothes on and his pockets full. Under the
scrutiny of the muscle bound officer he was a little intimidated
but he prayed he didn't let it show.

"Listen here," the Mr. T look alike started as Jeff gave his
undivided attention, "this here is my mother fucking cell block .
. . and I don't tolerate new jacks coming up here disrupting my
program." he was speaking slowly, matter of factly, his drawl

almost similar to that of a man high on heroin, "If you can't fight, or you're scared to fight, chances are you won't last long in the upper . . . I have a very low tolerance for pussies. If by some miracle, you're able to survive, in my house, there are specific rules that you will be required to abide by. Number one, your cell will be kept up to par at all times, I don't play no nasty shit. Number two, when I call the unit for chow, you will line up in two straight lines and there is absolutely no talking in my corridors. I don't care if the Warden wants to speak to you, keep your mouth shut until I say otherwise. If you ever disrespect me and make me look bad in them corridors or in the chow hall, I promise you, your ass is mine. Ask about me. They call me Big Bar. Do you have any questions?"

Jeff shook his head no and Big Bar smiled, a menacing smile.

"I'm putting you on the north side; twelve cell . . . welcome to the terror dome."

When big Bar went back inside the office he popped open the door to the north side and Jeff dragged the blanket that held all of his belongings through the mesh gate and into the cellblock.

Jeff's ears were assaulted by a T.V. blaring in the dayroom and snippets of conversation.

"That nigga Vee is dumber than three strips of bacon-"

"We're going ten, put us down for a ten!"

"- her ass was fatter than a government check."

"Dum-dum always talking about some bacon, I'm starting to think he hungry or something."

To Jeff's right, through plexi glass he could see dudes standing around the television, and a small crowd was gathered around a table where a heated card game was underway. No one seemed to be paying Jeff any mind although everyone was aware that a new jack had just entered the premises. Jeff kept it moving, passing by a dude using the phone and another three guys waiting to use it, each person he passed regarded him with little or no interest.

'That wasn't too bad,' Jeff thought as he made it to the cell he was assigned to.

The cell area was a short hallway with cells on both sides numbered from one to thirty. Jeff looked around the small dingy cell which was marked by the number twelve. It wasn't more than eight feet in width and twelve feet from the front of the cell to the back. There was a window at the back of the cell covered by mesh, and a knob that allowed you to open and close the window.

Jeff opened the small locker in the corner and a roach hauled ass as if it was in the Olympics trying to bring home the gold. A wave of nostalgia washed over Jeff as he regarded the rust ridden porcelain sink which boasted a matching toilet complete with no toilet seat. Jeff noticed a hole between-the toilet and the wall that someone tried to stuff with toilet paper. *Mice???*

'Oh hell nah!' Jeff thought as he stood there analyzing his new interim residence.

"Ayo! Where you from?"

Jeff was startled! He quickly turned toward the intruder prepared for whatever.

The dark skin dude had waves in his hair going to the side and he was standing just inside Jeff's cell.

Jeff took a deep breath and exhaled, "Man, you can't be

just running down on me like that," he said staring at dude.

The guy stared back at Jeff as if he had some serious questions and he thought he could find the answers in Jeff's eyes.

"Okay," the guy said after a pause, but he made no move to leave, "you're right and I stand to be corrected. My name is Chill and I'm from Brooklyn... Brownsville. What's your name and where you from?"

'This nigga is trying me,' Jeff thought, but he kept his cool because there was a chance he could've been wrong.

"Jeff, man. My name is Jeff! I'm from South Jamaica, Queens."

For the first time Chill smiled and Jeff didn't know if that was a good thing or a bad thing.

"Freeze is gonna be mad. Big Bar put you on the wrong side, ya'll Queens niggaz are deep on the other side-- over here you don't got nothing coming." Chill said looking Jeff up and down.

"I hear that." Jeff responded, not fully understanding where Chill was going with the conversation.

"What that nigga talking about, Chill?" a voice called out from the hallway.

"Shit! I think he trying to get on the other side with Freeze." Chill said getting comfortable and leaning against the door frame.

"Oh he's from Queens?" another voice asked.

"Basically!" Chill responded.

Jeff thought about the gem star he had stashed between his butt cheeks and finally understood the seriousness of what Rondu had told him.

"I think that's the nigga that broke Big House' jaw in Mod six." the first voice ventured.

Chill looked at Jeff with a smirk, "You had a fight with somebody in Mod six?"

Now Jeff was smiling, he was happy that somebody knew about what happened between him and Big House. Maybe now they would leave him the hell alone.

"If you want to call that a fight," Jeff spit like he was saying something slick.

"You don't get no brownie points for no play ground fight," Chill shot back, he didn't like Jeff's change of demeanor, "Mod six is a fuckin' playground, this here is the real deal nigga! You are now in shark infested waters-- eat or get ate! Remember what I told you."

Chill walked out of Jeff's cell obviously unhappy that he couldn't shake Jeff up.

Jeff quickly dug inside his pants and retrieved the match book that held the gem star from between his butt cheeks. He slid the razor inside his front pocket so he could have easy access to it. When no one else approached his cell, Jeff proceeded to make up his bed. He did so in a way that he was always able to see the front of the cell. It wasn't that he was scared, he just wasn't taking no chances.

CHAPTER 21

Shakim leaned against the wooden desk smoking a blunt filled with nothing but purple haze in it. The little scare he had with his uncle shook him up enough for him to abandon the quick high that he was afforded from crack cocaine. Besides, the life that Raheem had turned him on to was far more interesting than living the life of a person about to be turned out on drugs. It was an easy choice, and the fact that his man Boogie had recently got locked up for guns and drugs made it that much easier.

Now Shakim was up in the Marriott tricking off with two strippers that he managed to lure from Gordon's strip club just the night before.

Mahogany and Stacey were going hard in the fourth round, with Mahogany being the aggressor using a strapped on dildo and penetrating Stacey from behind. Stacey had her face on the bed looking up at Sha with dreamy eyes as she rested on her elbows with her ass wiggling in the air trying to match the intensity of Mahogany's back door assault.

This was Shakim's personal celebration for closing yet another deal. Thanks to his uncle Raheem, Sean Howard, and Skip over at Chase Manhattan bank, Shakim was the proud owner of another income property.

He stood in the hotel room in his boxer drawers with his

diamond crusted Mickey Mouse piece hanging from its platinum chain, exhaling haze smoke from his nostrils as he did the math. The building was at 100% occupancy at the time of purchase... with six apartments and rent being $1,500 a month for each unit, that came out to $9,000 a month. Raheem contracted a company that would handle the management; maintenance, rent collection, and the basic overseeing of the property-- a service that would set Sha back $4,000 every month after Raheem received his cut. Simple math, Shakim would receive a free five grand a month and he wouldn't have to so much as lift a finger.

Then with Raheem ending the beef he had with Steve, Shakim had free reign of the hood. He no longer needed to don bullet proof baseball caps and vests, nor carry around the heavy artillery that would've wound up sending him to prison probably for the rest of his life.

Mahogany lost the strap on dildo and was now giving Stacey the pleasure of returning her favor. Stacey was caressing and sucking on Mahogany's breast, giving each one equal attention.

Shakim reached inside his boxers and began to play with himself. The sounds alone that the girls were making had him ready for the next round. He placed the remainder of the blunt in the ashtray and went to join the party.

"Okay daddy," Stacey said as Sha came out of his boxers, "for a minute there I almost thought we weren't making you happy."

"No, his lazy ass thought he was gonna stand over there and referee for half the night. Get your ass over here and get back in the game!" Mahogany ordered, grabbing Sha by his erect penis.

At two grand for one night, Shakim wasn't putting up any resistance. Absolutely none at all.

Tasia left the house looking good enough to eat! She was wearing a black Dolce and Gabbana skirt set with black and gold Chanel shoes. She wore a gold blouse under her jacket and a black and gold Chanel bag to accessorize her outfit.

Tasia was on her way to work but she also needed to check on her car, and she planned on taking an extended lunch break about 11 o'clock so she could go and visit Jeff.

As usual, Mrs. Peterson was keeping herself busy by doing little stuff around her yard, but she stood and put her hands on her hips as Tasia was about to get into Jeff's Ford Explorer.

"Child! Where are your manners this morning?"

Tasia stopped and turned around, "Oh, I'm sorry Mrs. Peterson! I'm running late and there are just so many things on my mind, please accept my apology. How are you feeling this morning?"

"Praise the Lord, baby, I feel blessed. Now don't worry yourself to death, your mother told me all about that boyfriend of yours. You just put your faith in the Lord and everything will turn out for the best."

Tasia almost turned red out of anger! Yet, she managed to thank Mrs. Peterson for her kind words before getting into Jeff's truck and driving to work.

'I can't stand her' Tasia thought. She was in the visiting

room waiting on Jeff to come out but she was thinking about her mother. Tasia may as well had called CNN but they probably couldn't have done a better job broadcasting the news about Jeff to people all around the world.

'That was the last straw!' Tasia thought as she looked up and saw Jeff walking in her direction.

"Hi baby," she said getting up and giving Jeff a big hug and a kiss, " I miss you! You need to bring your ass home."

Tasia's presence alone was enough to erase all of the nonsense that Jeff was forced to encounter on a daily basis. Her hug was like water to a thirsty man stranded in the desert.

"I miss you too, Tay. Damn I miss you!" Jeff said inhaling her scent deeply. Jeff was so emotional that he almost didn't catch the look in Tasia's eyes.

"What's wrong?" He asked as they sat down across from each other.

"You mean besides my soul mate being taken away from me?" Tasia asked sarcastically.

"Yes boo, besides your soul mate being taken away from you . . . you got that look in your eyes." Jeff said.

It made Tasia feel warm inside that her baby could still read her like a book. She sucked her teeth, "It's my mother, man, that lady gets on my last nerve!"

"What happened now?"

"Nothing, it's just that every time I tell her something in confidence, she runs and tells the whole world."

"Then why do you keep telling her things that you don't want everyone else to know about?"

"Because she's my mother Jeff, I should be able to trust her. Now everybody in New York knows you're in jail for murder."

'So that's what this is all about,' Jeff thought.

"Boo, that's a small thing. I'm alright with people knowing what's going on with me, I'm not trying to hide anything. The thing I'm concerned with is you maintaining a healthy relationship with the woman that gave birth to you." Jeff said grabbing Tasia's hand.

"I'm not fucking with her no more," Tasia said stubbornly.

"Boo, that's you mother—"

"I don't care!"

Tasia hated when Jeff took her mother's side. Deep down she knew Jeff was right, but still, she felt as though Jeff would let her mother get away with murder.

"Don't be like that. Matter of fact, next time you come to see me bring your moms with you. Tell her I need to talk to her, okay?"

Tasia rolled her eyes, "Both of you make me sick. You're so intent on solving problems I wish you would solve your own."

Jeff massaged her hand in his," Just do what I asked you to do, and don't lose faith. Trust me Boo, when this is all over my problem will be resolved."

"It better be!" Tasia said pinching the back of his hand.

That's when officer Taylor came into the visiting room to make his rounds. When he passed by the row that Tasia and Jeff were sitting in Tasia leaned over the table talking excitedly.

"Boo, that's the guy I gave the three hundred dollars to!"

"Where?" Jeff asked looking around confused.

"The C.O. with the dreadlocks, his name is Taylor. He's from around our way."

"Get the fuck outta here." Jeff said smiling.

"Word to Dayday!" Tasia said.

Dayday was Tasia's little brother who was killed when a drunk driver ran him over with a tow truck.

The allotted time for visits on Rikers Island was one hour. C.O. Taylor let Tasia stay with Jeff for about three hours, until their butts started to hurt from sitting in those hard chairs for too long. They would've been allowed to stay longer but visiting hours were over and all the other visitors were already long gone.

CHAPTER 22

When Jeff got back to 4 upper after his visit it was almost count time. He was in a zone after seeing his soul mate and he was in no mood for bullshit. He was a man accused of murder and he needed time to think and try to figure a way out of the mess he was in without taking down the next man.

The guy Chill was on the phone again and as Jeff walked by, Chill looked him up and down with a smirk on his face.

'I'm gonna mess around and make an example out of him' Jeff thought as he entered his cell. The first thing Jeff did was check his stash inside the little hole between the wall and the toilet. The same hole that was stuffed with toilet paper to keep the mice out, that's where Jeff hid his weed and his gem star razor. It was still there! He grabbed the razor and slid it in his pocket before walking to the day room.

A slim dude from East New York named Supreme was channel surfing on the T.V. while a poker game was obviously breaking up. Guys were counting up and cashing in chips because it was almost time to lock down for the 4 p.m. count.

An old head with a friendly demeanor asked Jeff if he played poker.

"A little something," Jeff admitted.

When Supreme heard Jeff talking he immediately turned

his attention to the exchange.

"What's your game?" the old head asked.

"Kings and your low in the hole," Jeff responded, noticing the glances Supreme was casting in his direction.

"Okay, we play that. You young boys love all those wild cards. Me, myself, I prefer straight poker, nothing wild." The old head said, "By the way, the name is Bill!" He continued and held his hand out to Jeff.

"Dollar, dollar bill y'all!" One of the other poker players at the table sung as he stacked his chips neatly in front of him.

"I'm Jeff," Jeff said shaking Bill's hand.

"Well Jeff, you're welcome to play if you want to. We'll probably start the game back up after chow. You need two packs of A class cigarettes to get in, or the equivalent."

"I'll keep that in mind," Jeff said as the C.O. announced that it was time for lock down.

Out of Jeff's peripheral vision he peeped the dude Supreme looking all in his face with a look of hatred that Jeff couldn't understand. No one had reason to dislike him, they didn't even know him! Jeff just ignored the guy and made his way back to his cell for lockdown. Jeff's motto was: *'As long as a nigga don't put his hands on me...'*

After the officers made their rounds and conducted the count, Jeff twisted up some purple and blew a bone out the window in his cell. He used the baby powder trick he learned from Rondu to camouflage the smell, but the sharks weren't easily deceived.

"Ayo, Chill?!?" somebody was on their door calling down the tier.

"Yeah, yeah." came the response.

"You smell that?" the questioner asked in an outcry.

"Do I!"

"That shit is coming from twelve cell!" a voice close by exclaimed.

'Aint this some shit!' Jeff thought as he tried to fan the smell out of his cell.

"Ayo 'Preme, turn to Hot 97!" someone yelled out their door.

Jeff wanted to grab his radio and lay back and chill, but now the guys on their doors were blowing his high. He was paranoid.

Jeff tied up his white on white Air Force Ones and put his Yankee fitted on, pulling it down low.

'Fuck these niggaz,' he thought, studying his reflection in the scratched up mirror over his sink.

When the cell doors opened, Big Bar announced for everybody to get ready for chow.

Jeff stood in his doorway with one hand in his pocket on the gem star. He was high as a kite and his mind was operating on survival time. In his head he could hear the B.I.G. classic playing, *Niggaz bleed just like us.*

Dudes started crowding out onto the tier, and when Chill saw Jeff's disposition, something inside of him told him that Jeff wasn't a sucker. The untrained eye probably wouldn't see what Chill saw and this was obvious when Supreme stopped in front of Chill.

"Ayo, let's run up in this nigga's cell, I'm tryna smoke!" 'Preme said amped up and ready to go.

"Be easy, greasy." Chill said trying to buy time and figure Jeff out, "They're about to call chow."

Sure enough, Big Bar popped the door open and everybody started to file out.

"When we get back!" Supreme said loud enough for Jeff to hear.

Jeff slipped the matchbook with the gem star in it under his mattress because they had to clear a metal detector before they went into the chow hall.

They had fried fish with macaroni and cheese for dinner and Jeff tore it out the frame. A dude sitting next to him gave up his fish for a cigarette! The fish was so good that Jeff promised the guy two cigarettes to be delivered as soon as they got back to the block.

Jeff noticed on the way back that Chill and Supreme wouldn't allow anyone else to stand at the front of the line. No matter who got there first, they would force their way to the front of the line. Then when 4 upper passed Mod eight in the corridor, Jeff saw that Rondu was still playing the front of the line, so Jeff figured that the front of the line was reserved for the strong, those whom supposedly controlled the block.

Jeff was somewhere in the middle and that was cool with him. Rondu took his fist and hit his chest when he caught eye contact with Jeff, and Jeff returned the greeting. A few vets in 4 upper that knew how Rondu got down caught the exchange, and that was their first premonition that Jeff wasn't some sucker ass nigga.

Back at the block, Jeff went straight to his cell to retrieve his razor and the two cigarettes he had for the guy that sold him the fish. As soon as he stepped back on the tier somebody sucker punched him from his blind side! Jeff was dazed but he still had the gem star in his right hand. The two cigarettes were in his left hand and he let them fall as another figure advanced on him. Jeff threw a short left hook reversing the attack! Dude staggered back and the first attacker tried to slide in again from the blind side.

"Try to get him inside the cell!" somebody said from the back of the tier. It was Supreme! Jeff recognized his voice.

Jeff swung the razor at his attacker and the guy lifted his hand to block the blow. The skin on the back of ole boy's hand parted like the red sea.

"Oh shit! He got a razor!" The dude said retreating while he clutched at his wounded hand. He jetted into his cell looking for something to stop the bleeding.

Jeff advanced toward the second attacker and couldn't believe when the coward took flight! Dude ran into twenty-three cell and slammed the door behind him locking himself in.

Jeff turned his attention toward Supreme who was standing at the back of the tier, and he started walking in that direction. Jeff noticed that chill was nowhere in sight.

"Put the razor down and shoot a fair one!" 'Preme said standing in a combative posture.

'At least he got some heart and didn't run,' Jeff thought as he slid the razor in his pocket.

"What's going on back there?" Big Bar's voice boomed from the office.

"The new kid is tryna get five minutes with Preme!" a fat dude named Wop yelled.

"Well why didn't somebody say something?" Bar said sounding amused, "Clear everybody out of the dayroom! The only two people I want in there is Supreme and the new kid."

Everyone gathered their things and filed out of the dayroom and Supreme followed Jeff into the arena.

It was called five minutes but Jeff only needed one to handle his business. Jeff was so mad about them playing him like he was soft that he beat Supreme into unconsciousness within the better part of sixty seconds. Big Bar had to break it up before Jeff killed the poor fella!

Jeff figured with a performance like that he wouldn't have to worry about nobody else jumping out there. He was wrong!

"Let me get 'im, Bar!" a guy named Country said while someone helped Supreme out of the dayroom.

Country pulled his shirt over his head and tossed it to the side, revealing a tatted up body swollen from daily workouts.

"You guys can do this all night for all I care, as long as you keep it clean. Whoever got next get on deck," Bar said.

Jeff was breathing hard but that was a good thing. His adrenaline was pumping! Jeff danced around as Country cracked his knuckles and flexed trying to intimidate Jeff.

Jeff treaded into shallow water and caught ole boy with a two piece! It happened so fast that Country didn't know what hit him.

"Okaaay... I'm reloaded!" Jeff yelled dancing around.

Someone laughed in the background but for the most part Jeff's performance wasn't what the spectators had anticipated.

When Country pulled himself together, Jeff hit him with another two piece, but this time Country was able to get a blow off. He caught Jeff with a head shot!

Country was on point now so Jeff stopped dancing and switched his style up. Country thought Jeff was tired and advanced in to attack but this was exactly what Jeff wanted.

When Country came in swinging, Jeff did his signature move, the one he used on Big House. He dipped to the side and shot a hard right straight to the chin. Like magic, Country was out on his feet!

Jeff watched the big fella hit the floor before raising his hands in the air and doing a victory dance around the room.

"Boy, you keep this up and they're gonna start calling you a knockout artist." Dollar Bill said matter of factly.

"Where Pana at? Panama!" someone was yelling, "Pana, come slow this nigga down!"

"I don't have no beef with dude," Panama said humbly.

"Nigga if you scared, say you scared!" Chill spit.

"I'm not scared of nothing on two feet!" Pana shot back.

"Panama!" Big Bar called out, "Let's go, I don't got all day."

Panama sucked his teeth and entered the dayroom. Jeff knew the guy didn't want to fight, plus he was getting tired anyway so he decided to take it light on dude.

They circled each other like caged animals! The look in Panama's eyes told their own story. There was no hatred there but one thing was certain, Panama wasn't afraid, and he was focused.

Jeff tried to trick him and faked like he was about to swing but Pana didn't flinch. It wasn't until Jeff threw his first punch that he knew he was in trouble. Pana brushed the blow away and tagged Jeff on the forehead! No stranger to the art of boxing, Jeff knew that was just a warning. Pana could've aimed lower and broke his nose! Jeff looked into Panama's eyes and nodded his head up and down in acknowledgement. Panama smiled in return.

On the low, Jeff didn't like that shit. He decided to go into a different bag of tricks. Panama's smile widened as if he read Jeff's mind.

Jeff extended his right arm out to the side in an attempt to distract, leaving only his left hand to defend his head and body.

Panama shook his head from side to side as if to say don't even think about it. Jeff ignored him and waited for an opening-- it was all about timing.

Pana shrugged his shoulders like okay; have it your way. Then he let Jeff see what Jeff thought he was looking for, and when Jeff dipped low to come back up and attack, Pana was right there making it rain! When the smoke cleared, Jeff was sitting on his ass... dazed.

Panama waited, and when Jeff was ready Pana helped him to his feet.

"That's it son, it's over," Pana said and then continued. "Everybody wanted to see what you were made of, and you showed them. You're three and one in the terror dome, that's a winning record, they gotta respect that."

Panama held out his hand and Jeff gave him dap.

"You're lucky I was tired," Jeff said, and they both laughed as they walked out of the dayroom.

CHAPTER 23

When the deal was complete and Shakim was officially the owner of the property at 169-11 Hillside Avenue, Raheem personally called and thanked everyone that was involved in making the deal possible. He thanked Sean Howard for taking time out from his busy schedule in order to appraise the property, and for giving valuable advice in regards to the highest price that should've been paid to obtain it. He thanked Skip over at Chase Manhattan for his expeditious handling of the loan application which was an essential element for the deal to go through. With Raheem's successful track record and ever growing portfolio, Skip was able to approve a substantial loan on short notice. Finally, Raheem called and thanked Tasia for being patient and answering his many questions as honestly as possible, and for ultimately getting the green light to sell for six hundred grand as opposed to six hundred and fifty even though that consequently meant that Tasia would receive a smaller commission.

"Okay guys," Tasia had said at negotiations, "you're short changing my commission now!"

Raheem shrewdly interjected, "It depends on how you look at it. Personally, my goal is to purchase at least twenty-four properties per year. If I'm satisfied with the way this deal goes today I promise you, Colossal Realty in general, and you in particular, will be handling a considerable amount of deals just like this one in the near future . . . matter of fact, I've been trying to line up a condo, preferably a two or three bedroom in the city or not too far away. You can start working on that immediately."

"Do you know what a two or three bedroom condo in the city is going to cost you?" Tasia asked, slightly amused.

"If I didn't ask, Ms. Brown, it's because I'm not concerned. We'll cross that bridge when we get to it." Raheem said almost defensively.

"Well excuse me!" Tasia responded in her gangsta girl way, displaying a beautiful smile, "In that case I got you, and we'll go ahead and close this deal out at six. As far as that condo is concerned, I think I got exactly what you're looking for."

Now Raheem was on his way to pick up Tasia so she could show him a few condominiums in Manhattan. Raheem was pushing a white 750i BMW that he copped five months ago, yet this was only his second time behind the wheel. The truth was, he didn't like to drive. He preferred to be chauffeured around so he could think without distractions, and he also enjoyed watching the things taking place in the world around him.

When Raheem pulled up in front of Colossal Realty, Tasia was already waiting for him outside. Raheem took one look at her and was instantly annoyed. He prided himself on his discipline, and he seldomly fell victim to lusting over a woman's beauty, but, my, my, my, Tasia was making it hard --- literally!

Tasia had on some pink hip hugger pants accented with a wide matching belt. This was worn with a mid riff-baring jacket that showed off her diamond studded belly ring. She glided into the passenger seat and Raheem's nose was immediately assaulted by an intoxicating fragrance that swept his discipline right out the window.

"Hi!" Tasia said getting settled in, "We can go straight and get on the Van Wyck Expressway. Do you know how to get to the Mid-town Tunnel?"

"Uh-huh. Take the Grand Central to the L.I.E. and ride it out." Raheem said keeping his eyes on the road.

"Yeah, we need to get to Central Park, there's two condos on the west side that I want you to see." Tasia said, shivering from the freezing air blasting from the air condition vents, "Why is it so cold in here?"

Raheem found that funny! He glanced at Tasia with a smirk before shutting off the AC.

"What?" Tasia asked noticing the smirk.

"I didn't say nothing" Raheem said keeping his eyes on the road.

"That look you gave me said enough." Tasia said rolling her eyes.

"My bad," Raheem said and then continued, "didn't mean to offend you. I was just thinking that you wouldn't be cold if you was covered up."

"Excuse me?" Tasia said looking at Raheem like he was crazy.

"Uh oh! I don't know what I was just thinking. Please don't pay me no mind, Ms. Brown, I was just tripping. I do that every now and then, say things I don't have no business saying."

"No, you said what was on your mind. You don't think I have on enough clothes Raheem? What, you some kind of Muslim or something? Would you prefer if I covered up with a blanket and wrapped a towel around my head, or should I just stay at home and cook and clean?" Tasia asked in a confrontational tone.

"Ms. Brown, if you want to cover up with a blanket, that's on you. At no time can I dictate how another person dresses. At the same time, your dress code is a form of communication. It's a representation of who you are or who you're trying to be. Real talk, when I see a sister wearing clothes that hug every curve and accentuate the parts of the body deemed to be sacred, it's not always easy to control my desires. The same may be true for you if men generally walked around wearing pants that outlined their private parts. Matter of fact, women would call that straight up disrespectful. Imagine a dude walking around drawing attention to a hard on." Raheem stole a glance in Tasia's direction and saw that she was smiling. Satisfied that he had her attention, he continued, "Dude would be labeled a stone cold pervert. Not only that but how can people expect to connect mentally with another person when, for the most part, we never make it past the physical? I'm a man, Ms. Brown and -"

"—Call me Tasia."

Raheem looked at Tasia and smiled. They were in line to pay the toll to go through the Mid-town tunnel. Raheem let the 7 series BMW creep with traffic, and a comfortable silence lingered until after he completed the transaction at the toll booth.

"Tasia …you're a very attractive young lady. You're smart, career oriented, down to earth- If I was around you long enough I bet I could go on for days pointing out your good qualities. But answer this …what's going to distinguish you from the lazy, gold diggin', hood rats that lack the morals and character of such women whom deserve both honor and respect? We know the difference between a policeman and a fireman because of their uniform. The same holds true with the cat and the dog, who doesn't know the difference between the two? The outfit you have on Tasia is nothing less than tantalizing, a part of me wouldn't want to see you any other way. But, then the other part of me, the part that holds women in general in high esteem, that part of me is mortified! And that's because you're a queen, just like my mother. But that outfit you're wearing is bound to have every male human being from the postman to the cokeman chasing behind you like a dog in heat. And make no mistake about it, dogs chase dogs, and a female dog is a bitch. So, now our queens are being reduced to bitches and they still don't have a clue how it's happening."

Raheem hated to come off as if he was preaching, but, he wanted Tasia to be able to weigh the pros and the cons of dressing provocatively.

Tasia was silent, except for the few times she had to instruct Raheem which way to go. Tasia led him to an underground parking garage and before they got out of the car she joked, "As long as I don't catch YOU wearing no spandex, highlighting your hardware, you and I are cool!"

They both got a good laugh from that.

The upscale building was located at 599 Central Park West. They rode the east side elevator up to the 7th floor and Raheem was already falling in love with the quietness of the complex. It was as if they were in the building by themselves. Tasia led the way to unit 7011 and it took everything in Raheem's power to unglue his eyes from her heart shaped ass. It seemed to be bouncing to a rhythm all of its own.

"Well, this is it." Tasia said inserting the card key into the slot and then opening the door.

They stepped into the foyer and Raheem marveled at the

black marble floor that was buffed to a high gloss. He waved at his own reflection before lifting his eyes and looking around in awe. To his left was a half bathroom.

"This is for the guest of course. Each bedroom has its own full bathroom, and the master bedroom's bath area boasts his and her sinks, separate stand up shower with mosaic tile, deep garden tub, closet space, the works!"

Tasia transformed into the gracious host. She took a few steps into the unit, "As you see you have plenty of room . . . to the right we have a state of the art kitchen complete with sub zero freezers, high and low granite counters, if your culinary skills are up to par then this is definitely a room to be proud of. Tucked away behind the kitchen you'll find the laundry room, nothing extraordinary but you'll note you can enter the unit through the laundry room by using that door right there. Or it can be used for the hired help, it's your perogative."

Tasia walked back through the kitchen and crossed over to the dining room. There was a huge glass table situated in the middle of the room with eight matching chairs arranged in pairs on every side.

Tasia walked further south and made a left into a family room.

"This here is a cool out room, A.K.A the family room. You have the 40" plasma which is trademark throughout the unit. This area rug is comfortable enough to sleep on," Tasia said squatting down to run her fingers across the material, "The sectional couch dominates both the east and the south walls and is upholstered with butter soft leather from Italy, another trademark throughout the unit. Through that door on the other side of the plasma is a walk-in closet, and through this door

147

on the Westside of the room is a full bathroom. You can get to bedroom #1 through this bathroom, there's two ways in and two ways out." Tasia continued as she led the way through the bathroom and entered the bedroom.

There were two twin size beds separated by a nightstand, the signature 40" plasma was present, and a private balcony with two lounge chairs on it was the eye catcher.

Raheem stepped onto the balcony and enjoyed the beautiful view of Central Park.

"You won't truly appreciate this view until you experience it at night time." Tasia said and then continued, "Come on, you haven't seen nothing yet."

She led the way through another door that brought them full circle directly across from the family room. They made a left turn and cut back through the dining room and another left turn landed them in the Great room.

"Wow!" Raheem said shaking his head from side to side.

"I couldn't have put it any better than that myself," Tasia agreed, "This is what I like to call the activity room, you can call it whatever you like but officially it's called the Great room. On your east wall you have your bar/buffet, on your south wall is the entrance to bedroom #2, then you have the ever present 40" plasma…as you can see your west wall is glass from floor to ceiling giving you full view of the balcony and beyond that a beautiful view of Central Park, or you can always close the curtains for the feeling of complete privacy. The choice is yours. In front of the plasma on a different style rug is your glass coffee table flanked by two wing chairs. You'll notice the couch and the end tables also serve as a sectional, dividing the room. On the other side of the couch is a round game table with five chairs situated around it."

After briefly inspecting the bedroom, Raheem walked back through the Great room, past the bar/buffet and pushed through double doors that swung open from the center . . . he now stood in the master bedroom.

"This, Mr. Raheem . . ." Tasia said following him inside, "would be your personal domain. The only thing missing is a private kitchen, other than that it gets no better than this. Plasma, king-size bed, access to main balcony, breakfast nook, mahogany desk, his and her walk-in closets, the master bathroom is huge. The entire unit is prewired for the internet, surround sound systems, security -- absolutely no detail was ignored."

Raheem fell back on the king-size bed.

"Tasia . . . how much is this going to set me back?"

Tasia had such a beautiful smile. She leaned against the mahogany desk and hoped the price wouldn't send Raheem running for the hills.

"Five point four."

The silence that followed was enough to make Tasia believe that she could forget about that commission. Then, without warning, Raheem restored hope.

"Bring it down to four point nine and we'll both leave here happy, " he said standing up.

"Are you serious?" Tasia asked excitedly.
"Like HIV."

"Oh Raheem, thank you!" Tasia said running to him and smothering him with a friendly hug, "This will be the second big deal I closed this week."

Raheem tried to think of ice-cream, algebra, basketball, anything to stop his manhood from rising! Tasia was like a plague, he needed to avoid her.

When she released him and stepped back, clapping her hands together excitedly, Raheem was relieved.

'Keep it up,' he thought, willing his heart beat to slow down, *'she gonna make me put this dick on her!'*

CHAPTER 24

Jeff had a busted lip and a speed knot on the right side of his head but other than that he was fine. After lock down he sat on his bunk with a cold rag on his head in an attempt to abate the swelling. Throughout the night dudes were on their doors clowning and recounting, blow by blow, the highlights of the three back to back fights. Jeff had to smile when someone compared his fight with Supreme to the bout between Mike Tyson and Michael Spinx.

"-less than ninety seconds. That shit was a commercial," someone yelled drawing a wave of laughter.

"Nah, you know what the funny shit was?" Supreme interjected showing he wasn't taking the ridicule to heart, "all that gangsta stuff Doughboy was spitting, he got cut and swore to God he was gonna bleed to death! That nigga was crying like a bitch!"

"I aint gonna front, it looked like he tried to take Doughboys whole hand off! What that fool had a scalpel?"

"I don't know what he had but he split that niggas shit!"

Jeff fell asleep in all of his clothes. He woke up when he heard the doors to the cells opening, it was breakfast time. Jeff quickly got up and stood in the doorway of his cell with his hand gripping the gem star. Most of the guys were preparing to go eat, but Panama came over with his hand extended and gave Jeff some dap. Even Chill, after observing the knot on Jeff's head, asked if he was alright.

"No doubt," Jeff responded humbly.

"That's what's up," Chill said and then continued, "Men respect men, and more-less, you held your own like a man. It wasn't nothing personal."

From then on, Jeff was basically established on 4 upper. He ended up giving Chill, Panama, Supreme, and the guy Country a sample of the purple haze he had and they let bygones be bygones. The dude Doughboy went ahead and reported the cut on his hand claiming a sharp edge on his locker was the cause, but the administration wasn't buying that. After receiving medical attention Doughboy never made it back to the block, instead an officer came and retrieved his property. Later on that day Jeff played a little bit of Poker, but, he stayed on point. He was watching dudes with his good eye.

When an opportunity presented itself, Jeff called Tasia. She was excited about the commission she made off of the two deals she recently closed, also she told Jeff she had something important to tell him. No matter how hard Jeff pressed, Tasia wouldn't give him a clue as to what it was she had to tell him. Jeff just had to wait until he saw her.

The next day was a Sunday and Jeff was one of the first people called for a visit. When he walked out onto the dance floor he was surprised to see Tasia and her mother sitting there waiting on him. Jeff smiled so hard that his face started hurting!

"Hey, Mommy!" he said as Tasia's mom got up and gave him a big hug.

"Oh my goodness, they got the vegetable man locked in

a cage like an animal," Mrs. Brown said holding him tight.

Over her shoulder Jeff saw Tasia shaking her head. "The vegetable man is alright, how are YOU doing?" Jeff asked.

"I can't complain, Jeff. Some days are better than others."

Jeff gave her a kiss on the forehead and then turned to Tasia, "if you don't get your butt up and give me a hug..."

"That's right, Jeff, get her!" Mrs. Brown instigated.

Tasia rolled her eyes but she complied, giving Jeff a little tongue before sitting back down.

"What happened to your head?" Tasia asked, eyeing suspiciously what was left of Jeff's speed knot.

"Nothing," Jeff said massaging the small bump on his head.

"What do you mean nothing?" Tasia asked getting closer for a better look.

Tasia's mom put her glasses on, which were hanging from a chain around her neck, and did her own assessment, "baby, that boy been fighting."

Tasia gave Jeff a look that communicated disappointment.

"Come on Boo, don't start. We only have an hour to see each other and I'm not trying to waste it arguing. Let it go for now."

Tasia sucked her teeth and sat back in her chair, and Mrs. Brown was looking at Jeff with an expression that said *'well, what are you going to do now?'*

Jeff was use to Tasia and her moody ways so he just left her alone because he knew it would blow over.

"Mommy, let me ask you a question," he said turning his attention to Mrs. Brown, "what's your definition of a friend?"

The question caught Tasia's mom off guard and that was evident when she repeated the question.

"My definition of a friend?"

"Yep," Jeff said, giving her his undivided attention.

"Well, first of all, a friend is somebody you can trust, that's first of all, because without trust there is no friendship. Second, a friend is someone who loves you for you, period. It's someone who has your back whether you're right or wrong, but when you are wrong they have enough sense to tell you you're wrong."

Jeff was smiling, nodding his head in agreement.

"Some people won't say shit! You could be dead wrong and they'll know you're wrong but they won't even tell you. What kind of friend is that? A friend will let you know when you're wrong. In church we say a friend is someone who reminds you of God, and Godly things, but, my Mama use to tell us that a friend is a person who treats you right. I'll never forget what she use to tell us, she said baby, love the people who treat you right, and forget about the ones who don't."

"Okay, now wait," Jeff said holding up a finger, "I don't mean to cut you off but let me ask you this... I know you love Tasia, that's your daughter and you brought her into this world, but, do you consider her your friend?"

Tasia's mom had a look on her face like she just got caught doing something she wasn't suppose to be doing. Jeff had baited poor Mrs. Brown into a trap, and Tasia was waiting to hear her response.

"Well of course I consider Tasia my friend," Mrs. Brown said draping her arm around her daughter, "Tasia is my baby."

Now Jeff was looking at Tasia with a look that said, *I rest my case.*

"Why are you looking at me?" Tasia asked innocently.

154

"Because I want you to talk to your mother. Communication brings about understanding."

Tasia couldn't believe that Jeff was putting her on the spot like that, but, she sighed and addressed her concerns. "Ma, you know I love you, right?"

"Of course baby, and I love you too!"

"Well, you said a friend is somebody you could trust, but, it's like I can never tell you anything. Every time I tell you something in confidence you betray my trust-"

"Baby, that's not true."

"It is! I told you about Jeff being locked up and I specifically asked you not to tell anybody. You promised you wouldn't tell nobody, and then you turned right around and told Missy, you told Mrs. Peterson and God knows who else."

"But Tasia, they were going to find out anyway,"Mrs. Brown responded lamely.

"That's not the point Ma, I trusted you."

"Well I'm sorry. I don't know what the big deal is anyway, that was only one time-- it slipped."

"Ma? What about that time I told you about the problem Jeff was having with his feet, you promised not to say nothing. Then you turned right around and told him what I said, I would never do that to you!"

"And you're right baby, I was wrong for telling Jeff that his feet stink, but that don't mean that I don't love you. I would die for you! If God gave me a choice right now, me or you, I would tell him to take me. That's my biggest downfall, your mother has a big mouth! But I promise you, I swear on Dayday's grave I'm going to try my best to keep my big mouth shut. It's going to be hard, but I'm going to try. That's all I can do."

Tasia leaned over and gave her mother a hug and then capped it off with a kiss on the cheek, " I love you regardless! Big mouth and all," Tasia said before winking her eye at Jeff.

"I love you too, Baby!" Mrs. Brown said, meaning it from the bottom of her heart.

Shortly after that, visitation time was up. Officer Taylor wasn't working so an extended visit was out of the question.

"Boo, what you said you had to tell me?" Jeff asked as they said their goodbyes.

Tasia almost felt guilty about the lie she was about to tell, but, she needed to influence Jeff to try harder to make it back home. All he needed was a little motivation.

"Baby, I missed my period," she said in an award winning performance.

"What?"

"I think I'm six weeks pregnant..."

For a moment, Jeff's expression was enough to break Tasia's heart and she felt really bad but it was too late to turn back.

"That's why you need to hurry up and tell them people the truth so you can come home."

Suddenly Jeff was stressed out. Tasia may have had good intentions and she may not have meant to cause any harm, but, at the end of the day it was Jeff that was the victim. He was a victim of the games that people play.

CHAPTER 25

The Criminal Court building at 125-01 Queens Boulevard was a place where serious business was conducted. It was a dreadful place masked by a dignified exterior. The impressive architectural structure of the building with its sprawling corridors and shining floors encompassed on one side by glass walls were a stark contrast to the cramped holding pens obscured in the bowels of the edifice . . . holding pens that were intimately attached to dreadful court rooms that would otherwise serve no purpose . . . holding pens that held trustworthy stock and what shrewd investors considered to be a safe and wise investment . . . a place where hopes and dreams evaporated only to be replaced by despair.

Tasia sat in the courtroom marked K-10 waiting for Jeff's case to be heard. Jeff was scheduled for a bail hearing and Tasia prayed that the man in the flowing black robe would show mercy and grant the request.

When Tasia spoke with the lawyer, Mr. Slotnick, earlier that morning, two things became painfully clear. One, Jeff's chances at receiving a reasonable bail were slim to none, and two, time was running out. If Jeff didn't cooperate and tell the lawyer everything he knew, the state was going to force him to go the trial. Tasia was scared to think about what would happen if Jeff blew trial.

The good news was that forensics had confirmed that the blood of an unknown party was found at the scene of the crime-- that corroborated Jeff's story! Now if Jeff would come to his senses and give Chip up the whole ordeal could be over.

Tasia sat in the courtroom seething! This was a very serious matter, and she honestly didn't feel as if Jeff was treating it as such.

The courtroom was empty except for a few lawyers, the stenographer, an assistant district attorney, and four hoodlums that sat two rows in front of Tasia.

The clerk of the court rushed into the room with a sense of urgency and asked everyone to please rise. As everyone stood up, a small white man in his late fifties lumbered into the court and took his place behind the massive bench.

"Please be seated," he muttered once he was settled in. The clerk of the court began to call cases from the calendar.

"Docket #305 cr8500, the people of the state of New York versus Jeffrey Wilson!"

When Jeff was ushered into the courtroom by a court officer, Tasia's heart almost skipped a beat. Mr. Slotnick stood at the defense table and he said a few words to Jeff before the assistant district attorney began to speak.

"Your honor, Josh Claiborne for the state,"

"Barry Slotnick for the defense, your honor."

The judge was studying some papers in front of him, "This matter is a request for bail . . . let me hear from the defense first."

"Thank you, your honor," Mr. Slotnick said stepping forward and speaking with clarity, "Sir, aside from the charges that he is accused of today, my client is a model citizen. He has absolutely no criminal history- he's never been arrested. He's employed at a produce market here in Queens as a cashier and stock boy, and his employment dates back more than five years. He's lived in the County of Queens his entire life and he currently resides with his girlfriend of four years who showed up today in order to offer support."

Mr. Slotnick pointed in Tasia's direction and everyone in the courtroom looked back at her. Tasia squirmed in her seat and noted in particular the stares she received from the four hoodlums.

"His mother wanted to be here also, your honor, but I assured her that it wasn't necessary as this hearing would only determine whether or not her son would be granted bail. The defendant is clearly NOT a flight risk, your honor, the defense request that he be released on his own recognizance."

The judge seemed to be considering Mr. Slotnicks spiel before turning to the assistant district attorney, "Mr. Claiborne?"

"Your honor, the defendant is accused of MURDER! The fact that he has never been in trouble before has no relevance in light of the seriousness of the charge.... I applaud him for being a model citizen in the past, for establishing a history of employment and such. However, a human being has been deprived of life, your honor, and that man—"

The assistant district attorney jabbed a finger at Jeff, "Jeffrey Wilson, was caught at the scene of the crime holding the murder weapon! With all due respect sir, the people of the state of New York request bail be denied."

Tasia felt as if her heart had stopped beating all together. She held her breath as she waited to hear the judge's decision. A dreadful silence hung over the room.

"Well," the judge said folding his arms across his chest, "I don't think this looks too good for the defense. I imagine the victim's family would be outraged to learn, given the circumstantial evidence presented by the state, that the person accused of killing their loved one somehow made it back to society. However, I'm a firm believer in the constitution, and I believe that every person has a right to a trial and that . . . a person is innocent until proven guilty. The request for bail is granted. Bail is set at $2 million!

If the defendant is able to make bail he is to surrender his passport if he has one and he is not permitted to leave the state of New York. Court is adjourned!"

Steve, Kaymel, Doonie and Blast left the courtroom walking not too far behind Tasia.

"That's crazy, they locked up the wrong dude!" Doonie said in disbelief, "That means homeboy that killed Green eyes is still on the street,"

"Yeah, but that nigga there is still guilty by association," Kaymel said.

"Are you sure he's not the one who killed Green Eyes?" Steve asked looking at Doonie.

"Didn't you hear what the fuck I just said?" Kaymel snapped, "That shit is irrelevant, Steve! I want you to follow that bitch and find out what you can, if she don't want to give up no information you already know what to do. I'm not gonna be the only one hurting around this mutha fucka, I want some get back!

If she don't wanna give up the nigga that killed Green Eyes then that bitch is gonna have to take one for the team."

Kaymel knew that Steve didn't like to be unjust, but he was mad and he wasn't thinking. Steve sucked up the admonishment and followed orders. He followed Tasia across the street to a restaurant called Pastrami King. Steve was in line right behind her, and when Tasia turned around, Steve started up a conversation. He was talking fast and he got right to the point because he needed to keep Tasia's attention… her life depended on it.

CHAPTER 26

$2 million! Jeff's bail was so high it was as if the judge didn't give him a bail at all. The guys in the bullpen with Jeff said as much.

"Damn son, he gave you a ransom!" a guy name Bookoo said.

"No bullshit! He may as well not even gave you a bail." Bookoo's codefendant Chris added.

"I wouldn't say that because if he gets a bail bondsman he only gotta pay 10%," Bookoo stated as if he just dropped a jewel.

His codefendant Chris was sitting on the hard bench baffled trying to figure that one out, "How much is 10% of two million?" He finally asked.

"Chris, you's a damned fool!" Bookoo said and everybody fell out laughing.

"Man, you know I aint good with percentages," Chris said slightly embarrassed.

Bookoo was looking at him trying to determine if he was serious, and when he was convinced that he was, Bookoo told him the answer.

"Damn!" Chris said, "Two hundred thousand is still a lot."

Nobody knew and understood this better than Jeff did. There was no way in the world he was going to be able to make bail. He was bamboozled by the judge. Hoodwinked! All of that foolishness believing in the Constitution and every person being innocent until proven guilty was nothing but hogwash. That joker turned right around and gave him a $2 million bail as if he had money like Leona Hemsley.

When Jeff made it back to C-74 he was mentally brushing his shoulders off. *'Shit, it is what it is,'* he thought trying to stay positive.

Arriving back at 4 upper he found the block bustling with activity. Chill was on the phone as usual, a poker game was in full swing, and a little cutie pie C.O. named Ms. Hodges was in the office playing the latest CD by Mary J. Blige'.

'Damn, shorty is thicker than a mutha fucker,' Jeff thought as he made it to his cell.

The first thing Jeff did was check his stash to make sure everything was still there. Next, he took off the clothes he wore to court and threw on a Roberto Cavalli button up shirt with Diesel jeans. He was just about to go see what was happening at the poker table when Chill popped up in front of his cell. Tapping lightly on the door as a sign of respect he waited until Jeff acknowledged him before stepping inside the cell.

"What's good Kid, I see you went to court today."

"Yeah, I had a bail hearing," Jeff said sitting down on his locker.

"So you're outta here?"

"Hell no! That cracker gave me a $2 million bail,"

"Say word,"

Chill shook his head sadly as if he felt Jeff's pain.

"I'm sorry to hear that son, but anyway, I was trying to see if you wanted to sell some smoke."

"What you trying to get?" Jeff asked pulling out the small baggie half filled with haze.

"What you gonna give me for a carton of Newports?"

"Something proper," Jeff said pulling apart the sticky bud.

Rondu had just brought him a half ounce the night before on the medication run, and Tasia was suppose to see C.O. Taylor with some more money for yet another supply. Rondu was looking out for real, plus Taylor was in love with Tasia so his sucka for love ass was willing to look out for Jeff just so he would be able to interact with Tasia.

"You don't be getting no dog food?" Chill asked, prompted by an itty bitty monkey he had on his back.

"Fuck is that?" Jeff asked.

'Oh, this nigga is green,' Chill thought, but aloud he answered the question, "Heroin."

"Oh, hell nah, I don't fuck around."

"If you knew what I knew, you would!" Chill said and then continued, "that dog food is bail money. You can make a thousand dollars off a gram, and a gram only cost about $80."

"Say word."

"Word," Chill said, not bothering to share the fact that he liked to take a toot every now and then.

"Let me think about it, but ultimately I need to discuss it with my people. You know somebody that can move it if I get it?"

"Yeah, me!"

"Okay say no more. Let me look into it."

Jeff and Chill blew some haze together and then Jeff got on some solo shit listening to his radio and thinking about Tasia.

At one point Freeze came over to check on Jeff on the strength of Rondu. Ms. Hodges let them talk in the hallway.

"Ayo! When Bar come back on Monday I'm gonna have you pulled on the other side, you heard?" Freeze was saying.

Freeze was a big dude with a baby face. He was from Queens, but it was said that he was terrorizing dudes on the Southside of 4 upper regardless where a person was from.

"Nah, I'm good Fam. I done got comfortable over here," Jeff said in response to the suggestion.

"Are you serious? You gotta be the only one over there from Queens. What, them niggaz putting pressure on you?" Freeze asked in disbelief.

The rumor was that Queens niggaz couldn't live on the Northside of 4 upper, and the same went for Brooklyn dudes on the Southside. Consequently, Big Bar wouldn't normally put a guy from Queens on the Northside or a guy from Brooklyn on the Southside.

"Never that. I don't respond good to pressure," Jeff said in his humble demeanor, "It's just that I got settled in already, and I'm comfortable."

Ms. Hodges was ear hustling, "You're from Queens and you want stay on the Northside, that's a new one for me," she said.

"Ya'll trippin', the Northside is laid back," Jeff responded with a genuine smile.

Big Freeze looked at him suspiciously, "I think I'm gonna have to do an investigation on this," he said screwing up his face.

"I'll keep an eye on him for you, Reynolds."

"Yeah, you do that," Jeff agreed.

Before Jeff went back inside the cellblock, Ms. Hodges asked him his last name.

"Oh, Wilson? I got some mail for you," she said handing him two letters that smelled like perfume. One envelope had 'Photos enclosed', written on the back and 'Please Do Not Bend' on the front. Jeff rushed back to his cell, to open his mail.

CHAPTER 27

"You know he's innocent, right?"

When Steve said those words a million thoughts flashed through Tasia's mind. Her primary thoughts were *'who is this guy?'* and *'why the hell is he telling me this?'*.

Tasia normally would've brushed dude off, but Steve's words gave her hope. They were the exact words that she wanted to hear regardless of where they came from, thus she sat down and had lunch with the stranger.

"The guy who was killed was a good friend of mine," Steve said after they were seated, "and some very dangerous people have their minds set on avenging his death."

"Who are you?" Tasia asked looking up from her tuna melt sandwich that she just removed from the plastic wrapping, "I mean, what's your name and why are you telling me this?"

Steve was eating Pastrami on rye and he grabbed a napkin to wipe mustard from the side of his mouth, "My bad, my name is Steve," he said and then continued, "I know you're probably skeptical about me approaching you like this, but, the truth is that I think we can help each other."

Steve hadn't eaten all morning so he was attacking his sandwich with a vengeance.

"Help each other how?" Tasia wanted to know what he

knew.

"Well for one, your boyfriend may be in danger. There are—"

"Wait a minute! Why would Jeff be in danger, you said it yourself he's innocent!"

"Calm down, Shorty," Steve said studying the surroundings, "Take it easy and I'll explain to you what I know and then we'll figure out what we can do, okay? Now what's your name? I told you my name but I don't know yours."

"It's Tasia!"

"Okay Tasia, listen, it's like this . . . one of your boyfriends people killed my man Green Eyes. We don't know who dude is, but, if they can't find the person who actually pulled the trigger then they're going after the next best thing. We got people on Rikers Island right now ready to punish your man, but, me personally, I'm a fair dude, I don't wanna see your boyfriend get caught up if he don't got nothing to do with this."

Tasia instantly remembered the lump on Jeff's head.

"Well if you're a fair dude and you KNOW that Jeff doesn't have anything to do with your friend getting killed, then why the hell are ya'll fucking with him?"

"Tasia chill," Steve said glancing around nervously.

"Don't tell me to chill, ya'll need to fucking chill!"

"And that's why I'm talking to you, Tasia, if you'll just chill for a minute I'll tell you what we can do to straighten this out," Steve said trying to get ole girl to calm down and lower her voice.

Tasia was peeved! She couldn't even eat her tuna melt because she lost her appetite.

"Do you know who killed Green Eyes?" Steve asked.

"It was fucking Chip! Loud mouth Chip from Merrick!"

"Okay, that's what I needed to know. But, for real-for real, I don't even wanna see him get killed because it won't bring Green Eyes back. Between me and you, if we can find a way to make Chip go down for what he did, and at the same time get your boyfriend back on the streets, then both of our problems would be solved. Do you agree with that?"

"Hell yeah!"

"So it's up to us to make it happen. When you talk to Jeff don't mention nothing about this conversation. I'm gonna see what I can find out about this dude Chip and then I'm gonna get back at you. You got a cell phone number I can reach you at or something?"

Tasia gave Steve her cell phone number, her house number, and her job number.

When he left the restaurant her fingers were crossed and she was counting Steve as an ally. This was her way of keeping hope alive.

CHAPTER 28

They just had to play Aaron Hall's song, *'I MISS YOU'*! Jeff was laying on his bunk vibing! The headphones on his head were on full blast and he was looking at the pictures that Tasia sent him in the mail. One picture in particular tugged at Jeff's heart. It was a picture of Day-day, Tasia's little brother that was mowed down by a drunk driver in a tow truck on his 13th birthday.

'Damn!' Jeff thought as he remembered how excited Day-day was because he was finally about to become a teenager.

"I'm gonna be one of the big boys now, right Jeff? When I'm a teenager and I go back to my old school, the other little kids are gonna be sweating me, watch! And my mother probably gonna let me stay outside late on weekends, right Jeff?"

The questions were innocent! Day-day was just a kid excited about life, but, he never got a chance to live.

The morning that Day-day got killed was embedded in Jeff's memo forever, no matter how hard he tried he couldn't forget that morning.

"Noooooo!" Tasia screamed. She repeated this over and over again as she ran through the house blindly, knocking pictures off the wall and smashing any and everything that she could get her hands on. Jeff tried to subdue her and be there for

her but Tasia was past the point of no return. Her cries could be heard from the street as neighbors and strangers alike crowded around the scene of the accident. Distant sirens could be heard as a result of several calls to 911.

The man in the tow truck looked pathetic, his clothes in disarray his breath reeking of alcohol as he departed from the tow truck scanning the huge tree in front of Tasia's house. Neighbors followed his gaze and soon recognized the upside down, battered body of little Day-day as he swung back and forth with his foot caught between branches of the tree.

As the sequence of events dawned on the people, the front door exploded open and Tasia came rushing out of the house with a butcher knife held high as she searched for and found her intended target. Jeff was behind her at a safe distance looking for leverage to take control of the situation.

"Tasia no!" he yelled, but Tasia was already rushing toward the tow truck driver screaming, "He killed Day-day!"

Before the tow truck driver realized what was happening, Tasia had plunged the big knife deep into his right shoulder blade. She was raising the knife to strike again when Jeff grabbed her and pulled her away.

"He killed Day-day!" Tasia cried as Jeff struggled to take the knife away from her.

"It was an accident," Jeff whispered to her, sounding as if he was on the verge of breaking down, "It was a terrible, terrible accident."

The nosey ass neighbors just watched in horror as the scene unfolded. The tow truck driver lay on the ground clutching his shoulder, a flow of blood dripping from his fingers.

Meanwhile, Jeff and Tasia were fighting for possession

of the bloody butcher knife. No one had enough sense to help Jeff subdue Tasia, everyone kept their distance refusing to get involved.

Mrs. Peterson from next door had her eyes fixed on the lifeless body of Tasia's little brother as it remained hanging from the tree. All the blood had rushed to Day-day's head making him appear to be darker than he actually was. Mrs. Peterson covered her mouth with both hands and cried softly. Day-day was just a baby!

Suddenly Tasia stopped fighting with Jeff and let go of the knife. She turned to look up at Day-day as if there was a chance that he was still alive. Jeff allowed the knife to fall to the ground but he continued to hold Tasia firmly, lovingly, "It's gonna be alright Boo" he said in the most convincing voice he could muster, "Day-day is going to a better place than this --"

"Noooo Jeff, let me go!" Tasia cried, rocking back and forth, "Get off of me, he's not dead! We have to help him Jeff . . ."

Two police cars finally made it to the scene and the ambulance wasn't far behind. One of the officer's attention was instantly drawn to Day-day's body in the tree.

"There's a man down over here," another officer yelled, "Bring a stretcher, this guy's losing a lot of blood!"

Jeff turned his radio off and removed his headphones from his ears. Tears flowed freely down his face as he stared at the picture of a smiling Day-day holding a basketball.

"I miss you, baby bro' . . ." Jeff said before kissing the picture, "From God we came, and to God is our final return."

CHAPTER 29

Shakim maneuvered his Range Rover into the light traffic as they left Chase Manhattan Bank on Linden Boulevard near 204th street. Stephanie was sitting up front in the passenger seat while Raheem was in the rear reading back issues of Ebony magazine.

"Unc... you got a brand new 7 series BMW, why would you spend all of that money on a car and then don't drive it? That's crazy" Sha said looking at his uncle through the rearview mirror.

"That's what I have you for, nephew, you're my personal driver," Raheem responded with a smile. "As a matter of fact, stop by that Jamaican restaurant on Farmers, Genes, I'm in the mood for some Oxtails with peas and rice. And keep your eyes on the road before you mess around and crash."

Stephanie was up front laughing. Raheem liked Stephanie, he thought she was a good girl for his nephew. Sha just needed to open his eyes and see it.

"Listen to this ya'll," Raheem said before Sha could say something stupid, "Blacks account for nearly half of the roughly one million Americans living with HIV. Now you know that don't make no sense. That's exactly why you two love birds need to just go ahead and get married, and be committed."

"Wow" Stephanie proclaimed turning around in her seat ignoring the comment about her and Sha getting married, "You just read that in Ebony? Let me see that magazine."

While Raheem passed Stephanie the magazine he noticed Sha looking at him all crazy through the rear view mirror.

"What?" Raheem asked playing dumb.

Shakim just shook his head from side to side. He couldn't wait to drop both of them off.

"It says here, in 2002 HIV was the #1 cause of death for black women 25 to 34 years of age," Stephanie shared in disbelief.

Shakim wasn't with all the talk about HIV and AIDS. As far as he was concerned, none of those statistics pertained to him. But, Shakim was far away from the truth, in fact he was in denial. In his mind he still thought HIV and AIDS were gay related diseases, or that you had to be an intravenous drug user to contract the disease. He didn't know that among black females alone, roughly 78 percent of the HIV diagnoses were attributed to high risk heterosexual contact. Intravenous drug use accounted for 19 percent.

Never the less, without knowledge, people were often rendered powerless, and thus, while Stephanie and Raheem discussed HIV in the black communities, Shakim was thinking about his next ménage a trios.

Almost a whole week passed before Tasia found time to go pick up her car. James Carter had faithfully called her everyday, sometimes twice a day, to remind her to stop by his car lot. The car dealer was just happy to have a reason to call Tasia and he looked forward to seeing her again.

Tasia paraded onto the car lot in a pair of stonewashed E.C. denim jeans that hugged her ass-ets like tight drawers. Baby girl's swagger was on one million and every male she passed turned their heads to admire her beauty, and a few females too. Once Tasia made it inside the trailer that operated as the office for the dealership, she turned around to thank the guy who held the door for her and was shocked to see the older man squatting low for a better look at her ass.

"Fucking pervert!" she spit as the guy quickly straightened up with a silly grin on his face.

"Don't be mad at him," a guy outside yelled, "with an ass like that YOU need to be arrested-- somebody call 9-1-1!"

Tasia was steaming! She spun around to the receptionist and requested to see James Carter. While she was waiting she reflected on the conversation she had with Raheem. Raheem had been right, the way she dressed was a representation of who she was, and she couldn't expect to be treated like a lady if she continued to dress like a hoochie mama. Tasia vowed right then and there to dress more conservatively. She was going to demand respect by being a lady at all times and in every aspect.

"Hey Tasia, what's up? I'm sorry if I kept you waiting," James Carter said licking his lips and undressing Tasia slowly with his eyes. "You are truly a beautiful creature to look at, damn!"

"Boy, stop playing!" Tasia said in a friendly tone.

After all that James did for her, she wouldn't allow herself to flip on him.

"Where's my car at? You kidnapped my baby for five

whole days," she laughed.

James led Tasia to a blind side of the lot that couldn't be seen from the street and her Honda Accord was right there. It was next to a red SC430 Lexus Coupe that was calling Tasia by her first name.

"I have good news for you, and an offer you can't refuse," James said noticing the look in Tasia's eyes, "I have a customer ready to pay eleven grand for your Honda. If you take it, I'll subtract that away from the price of this pretty little thing right here," he said patting the Lexus affectionately.

"And what exactly is the price of that pretty little thing?" Tasia asked, hoping he gave her a good deal.

"Well," James said reverting into salesman mode, and forgetting momentarily his desire to be in Tasia's good grace, "This being a 2002 model with only 49 thousand miles on it, one previous owner... I can let it go for twenty-nine. Take away eleven and you can be the new owner for eighteen thousand dollars."

Tasia's eyes were wide open! James was right, this was an offer she couldn't refuse. Matter of fact, this would be her little treat in celebration of the two deals she recently closed.

"I can finance it, right?"

"Of course. And I won't make you pay no down payment, but, there's a $650 bank fee, plus you'll have to pay tax, tags, and motor vehicle fees."

Tasia clapped her hands excitedly, "let's fill out the paperwork before I change my mind."

"Let's go back to my office then," James Carter agreed, getting Tasia to lead the way so he could admire her thickness, "I told you I'd take care of you but you didn't believe me. I bet that ass will start believing me now."

James may as well had been speaking Arabic because Tasia wasn't hearing anything he said. She was too busy visualizing herself driving off the lot in her new drop top Lexus.

'If only Jeff could see me now, he would be so proud of me,' Tasia thought.

Just thinking about Jeff was almost enough to put a damper on her spirit, but then again, she knew that Jeff's first priority would've been her happiness. If he was there he would've encouraged her to buy the car, so that's what Tasia intended to do.

CHAPTER 30

Jeff didn't really want to, but, he went ahead and spoke to Rondu about bringing some heroin into the building. Jeff explained his desire to at least try to come up with some of the bail money. He figured if he could make a nice chunk, then his mom could put up the house and he could even get Alan to help out.

Rondu was on automatic, he didn't need no convincing at all! After doing his homework he found out that C.O. Taylor knew someone who would give him some half decent heroin for a hundred dollars a gram.

To start, Rondu and Jeff copped a gram apiece. While Rondu sold his drugs on his own, Jeff passed his off to Chill who packaged the drugs up in $50 portions. Off of one gram of heroin Chill was able to bag up twenty-six packages. $1,300!

Jeff wasn't tripping, he told Chill to give him $700 and keep the rest. The next day Chill gave Jeff $700 in cold cash.

"Man, where you get all this money from?" Jeff asked in amazement.

For real, the small stack of money was enough to make Jeff a little paranoid.

"What, you don't want it?" Chill asked.

"Hell yeah."

"Then don't ask no questions kid, you just do your part and let me do mine."

Chill didn't have to tell Jeff twice! Jeff jetted off the block when they called medication and gave Rondu the whole $700.

"You aint saying nothing slick, Jeff, I knocked mine off too!" Rondu said pulling out a knot of big face twenties.

From that moment on, it was poppin'! Jeff and Rondu jumped from two grams to a half an ounce. They drained so much cash out of the building that they started making 'outside' transactions. An 'outside transaction was when a person would have their people drop the money off to either Tasia or a person of Jeff's picking, and once the money was received that's when the person would receive the drugs. This was sometimes a slower process because of availability, but, within three weeks Jeff's seven grams was gone and he was $4,900 richer.

Jeff would sometimes mail his money to his mother or Tasia to hold for him and at other times he would take it to Tasia directly on the visit. When Tasia questioned him about the large amounts of money Jeff lied and said it came from selling weed. Tasia just told him to be careful, because she wasn't too worried about weed, but, had Jeff told her that the money came from selling heroin, Tasia would've had a heart attack.

C.O. Taylor continued to allow Jeff and Tasia to enjoy two and three hour visits and Tasia seldomly missed a visit. Just as Tasia expected, Jeff was elated when she told him about her new Lexus. Jeff- was actually proud of her because she was independent and he started calling her his GO GETTER!

His Go Getter was the one to convince Mr. Slotnick to take Jeff case. Actually, once Mr. Slotnick learned about the blood found at the crime scene that belonged to an unidentified person, he started to be optimistic about defending Jeff. Couple that with the fact that at least two other fire arms were discharged on that fateful night of the murder as was exemplified by the numerous case shellings found at the scene of the crime, and Mr. Slotnick had a strong belief that he might even be able to win the case.

The lawyers optimism was contagious and both Jeff and Tasia began to relax and let Jeff's situation take it's course. Tasia even went ahead and told Jeff that she had a miscarriage so he could stop worrying her to death about the baby.

As the months passed, Jeff and Rondu made a decent amount of cash, not enough to free Jeff, but enough so that they didn't want for nothing. Jeff even developed a rapport with a nurse whom he thought bore a strong resemblance to the R&B singer Keyshia Cole. Being that he was always coming out when they called medication yet he never received any meds, Jeff would sometimes stop by the nurse's station and kick it with the nurse for five or ten minutes. When he told Shorty that she looked like Keyshia Cole her smile went from ear to ear. It was obvious that she appreciated the compliment so, from that point on Jeff started calling her Ms. Cole. Babygirl was 23 years old and she told Jeff that she was from Harlem. He learned that she liked to read urban fiction, in fact she and Jeff read a lot of the same books and they would get excited talking about the good ones like the Gangsta Paradise series by Don John.

"24 Hours To Live was my favorite book in that series," Jeff said and then continued, "When Corleone came back at the end, the funeral scene? That was gangsta, I was feeling that ending."

"I didn't like when Lisa got killed," the nurse said frowning up her face.

Then on one occasion old girl told Jeff she could sing. When no one was around he tried to get a little sample.

"Let me hear something, Keyshia! You said you can blow."

"Noooo!" she said with that pretty smile, "not right here!"

"Then where?" Jeff pressed, smiling at her nervousness.

Shorty sucked her teeth, "I'll tell you what . . . here, put your name and number on this," she said handing him a clipboard.

"What the hell is this?"

"That's the list to take a HIV test."

"HIV test? I'm not taking no HIV test!"

"Why not? That way you can come down and hear me sing. I have an office in the clinic where they do the testing at."

"Oh," Jeff said smiling, "Since you put it like that, I don't see nothing wrong with giving up a little blood."

"You're crazy!" the Keyshia Cole clone said laughing.

And Jeff was laughing too, but, life isn't always a laughing matter. If Jeff only knew what the near future held in store for him, he probably would've laughed little and cried a lot.

CHAPTER 31

Now that Shakim had a pass in the hood, he relentlessly set out to sex every chick that stood on two legs! Baby boy was insatiable, and he particularly found the younger girls appealing to him the most. Shakim had no shame, he would creep off with chicks that was only fifteen or sixteen years old if he could get away with it.

"They must've put something in the similac because these young bitches are built like stallions!" Sha would tell anyone who would listen to him.

"True story, that little bitch Brenda got stamina like a grown ass woman!" he told Boogie one day before Boogie got locked up.

"You're a dirty ass dude, son, I know you didn't fuck that little ass girl," Boogie said in disgust.

"Little girl?" Sha asked in disbelief, "If she's old enough to have a baby then she's old enough for me to put this dick on her. Don't be mad at me, be mad at her baby's father, he started this shit."

Boogie just shook his head because he knew that Brenda was barely fifteen years old.

"True story," Sha continued defending his position, "her little ass got SuperHead beat, plus she take it in the ass. Man, she taught ME some new tricks!"

Boogie was just glad that he didn't have any little sisters, he would have to kill Shakim.

Still, ever since Boogie got locked up Shakim had managed to stay crack free, and that was a good thing. Almost two months had passed since he smoked his last woolie. Tamika was strong enough to stop when Sha stopped, but unfortunately, Shelly was the one that fell victim to the highly addictive drug.

One day Shakim was driving down Guy R. Brewer boulevard on the late night when he saw Shelly under the truss near 116th avenue. This was an area that crack heads occupied to turn tricks so they could have money to get high. Shakim was in the Maxima and Shelly must've not recognized the car because she approached the passenger side trying her best to walk seductively.

"Looking for a date?" she asked in a husky voice before she recognized the person behind the wheel to be Sha. Her facial express instantly registered surprise and then anger.

"Nigga, that's fucked up how you did me!" she yelled standing there with her hands on her hips.

Sha noticed the dirty ass clothes she had on and it looked like she was in desperate need of a shower, yet she was standing there as if she still had swagger.

"How I did you, Shelly?" Sha asked as if he didn't have a clue as to what she was talking about.

"You know I was backed up on my rent and I barely had enough money to feed my son. You left me for dead and now I'm out here humiliating myself just trying to survive."

"Bitch, you on that glass dick! You think I'm stupid? You're out here sucking and fucking so you can get high. Where the fuck is your son at?"

The hurtful words pierced Shelly's armor like hollow tip bullets! Shakim had pulled her card, and although he was right, deep down Shelly knew that he was at least partially responsible for her situation. He was the one who introduced her to smoking woos. She vowed to herself that she would get him back if it was the last thing she did, but, for now she needed him. "Buddy is with my mother, Sha, I have to pick him up in the morning. But I'm glad I ran into you because I don't have no money. Come on and bless your girl so I can get off this corner, you know this aint even me."

"Bitch, don't give me that bullshit," Sha said with a smirk and then continued, "I got $20 for you, but, I work hard for my money. It's only right you work hard for yours."

Shelly smiled, but her heart was filled with a hatred that she never knew before. As she opened the passenger door to get inside the Maxima all she could think about was some get back.

'*You just wait,*' she thought as she prepared to suck Shakim's manhood, '*I'm gonna bake your ass a cake, you done went and crossed the wrong bitch this time.*'

Shelly took the whole jump-off in her mouth while she cupped and massaged the balls. A classic deep throat move.

"Damn! I was in denial. I forgot you had crazy skills on the mic," Sha said, laughing at his own joke.

Shelly just continued to do what she set out to do. In her heart she knew that she would be the one who had the last laugh. It was just a matter of time.

CHAPTER 32

Jeff's eyes were low but his mind was on a higher plane as a result of the strawberry dro that he just finished smoking. He was at the poker table trying to bluff and outthink three opponents, but, mostly Jeff was bullying the table. Even when he didn't have a promising hand he would bet high, causing those with short money to fold their hands early if they didn't have anything.

"Man, I'm not trying to let none of yall wait around and catch," Jeff said when the guys would complain, "You gotta know when to roll 'em and know when to hold 'em."

In particular, Jeff was looking to get some get back on the old- head Dollar Bill. Dollar Bill suckered him into a big ass bet and then crushed him. They were playing kings and your low in the hole and Jeff caught three wild cards off the rip. He had a king and a pair of deuces. He turned up a deuce, the next man turned up a jack of heart, Dollar Bill turned up a five of spade, and the last man turned up a three of diamond. Jeff was regulating the hand because he was the dealer.

"Jack bet," he said pointing at the jack which was the highest card on the table.
"Jack bet five!" the guy said tossing five chips in the pot.

Everybody saw the bet but when it got to Jeff he raised.

"Five plus five more, let's make this interesting," Jeff said tossing in the extra chips.

"Here we go with the bullshit," one of the guys complained, everybody was in.

Jeff dealt the cards. The guy with the jack face up received a four of diamond, Dollar Bill caught an Ace of heart, ole boy with the three of diamond showing was blessed with a king of club, and Jeff turned up a queen of spade for himself.

"Okay Dollar, it's on you with that big ass Ace."

"Shit, I'll keep the bet at five," Dollar said.

"The last bet was ten chips," Jeff reminded him.

"Well I'm keeping it at five," Bill said tossing in his chips.

Dude who just got a king was looking at Jeff crazy, he knew what was about to happen so he just folded his hand with a wild card showing and all.

"That's right run, I'm about to bully the hand. I think I can buy this one," Jeff said counting out fifty-five chips, "Five plus fifty is the bet."

The next man folded too but Dollar Bill called the bet.

"Okay Dollar, you don't wanna get out the way huh?" Jeff asked with a smile.

He dealt the cards turning up a ten of diamond for Bill and a seven of spade for himself.

"I check," Bill said watching Jeff closely.

Jeff looked in the old-heads eyes trying to read them.

"Check good," Jeff said rolling the cards. Dollar Bill caught a five of heart and he now had a pair of fives on board, Jeff caught an eight of club.

"Pair of fives check," Bill said without hesitation.

"Check good," Jeff agreed, "How you want your last card, up or down?"

"Go 'head and turn it up, youngin'" Dollar Bill said smoothly.

"Oh, you got yours already, huh?" Jeff asked turning up a six of heart, "I know one thing, you better hope I don't catch because I'm going to the moon!"

Jeff took his card down and quickly began to mix his three hole cards together in his hand. Dollar Bill picked up his stack of chips and began counting them.

'This nigga got five Aces,' Jeff thought as Bill continued to count his chips.

Jeff had yet to look at the card he just caught but he was starting to think that Bill was bluffing. When Bill finished counting his chips, he took one chip and tossed it in the pot.

"I bet a chip," he said, looking at Jeff as if he dared him to raise.

"What?" Jeff yelled in surprise, "Man, you better hope I didn't hit."

Jeff had his cards one behind the other and he slowly began to check to see what he hit. In the front was the two of heart, as he squeezed the cards apart the king of diamond came into view, and as he ever so slowly continued to squeeze the cards apart Jeff's heartbeat quickened. He hit a queen of heart giving him five queens!

"I gotta go Dollar, I'm sorry. One chip plus I raise you —I'm all in!" Jeff pushed all of his chips next to the pile on the center of the table.

"I call," Dollar Bill said pushing his chips near the pile, "I got five Aces!" and the old head turned them pretty little arrowheads over.

"Damn!" Jeff said, "You caught me! Busted my head to the white meat. I had to go, I had five queens."

"And you still got 'em" Dollar Bill retorted.

Now Jeff was looking for some get back but he couldn't hit for nothing. They were in between hands when Big Bar called his name.

"Wilson! They want you down in medical, make sure you have your I.D. card."

'Oh, okay,' Jeff thought as he jetted to get his I.D.

When he made it to medical there were only two other inmates in the waiting area and Jeff spotted little Ms. Keyshia Cole pushing a cart filled with prescriptions toward a room off to his right. Shorty smiled when she saw him and Jeff felt a little guilty because he knew Tasia would have a fit if she saw how he was flirting with the nurse.

A couple of minutes passed before the nurse came into the waiting area with a clipboard. She was going through formalities.

"Wilson? Is there a J. Wilson here?"

"Yeah, that's me," Jeff said following ole girl's lead.

"Follow me."

'Gladly,' Jeff thought as he followed her to the back. They walked past a host of officers and hospital staff until she brought Jeff into an exam room and closed the door behind them.

"What took you so long to come down?" she asked as if she had an attitude.

"They just called me and I came right down. What are you talking about?"

"Boy, I called for you over an hour ago," she said bringing a stool over for him to sit on.

"That's crazy. I wonder why they played me like that."

"Don't worry about it," Shorty said as she rolled a portable work station over to where they were, "I'm going to give you the oral test. There's actually two ways I can do it, I can draw blood or we can use the swab. The swab is easier so I'm just going to do it that way.

"Oh yeah? I came down here to hear you sing and you got me up in here taking an AIDS test. Ms. Cole, you're something else."

Another nurse came into the exam room then and walked over to one of the overhead cabinets. Keyshia Cole told Jeff to open his mouth and she placed a swab inside his mouth. By the time the other nurse found what she was looking for and left the exam room the procedure was over.

"Can I hear you sing now?" Jeff asked grabbing Shorty by her hand.

Her smile lit up the room, "What do you want me to sing?"

"Sing whatever you feel is appropriate," Jeff said, feeling a strong connection between him and Shorty.

She thought for a moment, and then her beautiful voice penetrated the confinement of the small exam room.

"I will love you anyway . . . even if you cannot stay, I think you are the one for me-- here is where you ought to be."

Her rendition of Sweet Thing had Jeff caught up in the rapture. Babygirl could sing for real!

After she tore it down, she and Jeff talked for a while and then it was time for Jeff to go. The other nurse had come into the room again and that was the cue.

Later that night Jeff found himself in deep thought

thinking about the nurse. That was probably because he was lonely and his emotions were overly sensitive but, he knew that it was Tasia that he was suppose to be thinking about. Tasia was his soul mate. She was out there alone and probably feeling just as lonely. What if Tasia was thinking about someone else just like Jeff was a moment ago? The thought alone was enough to make Jeff sick. He went to sleep with one person on his mind and that person was Tasia.

Three days later they called Jeff back down to medical. He got to see Ms. Cole and they spoke a bit, but another nurse was handling the test results.

When Jeff was called into exam room #2, for some reason he was feeling kind of nervous. He was told to have a seat and one of the first things he noticed was a huge picture of a person in a body bag. The caption D.O.A. in bold red letters crossed the body bag diagonally. Above the pictorial it read: YESTERDAY HE TOOK HIS MID-TERMS, TODAY HE'S TAKING HIS FINAL EXAM! And under the pictorial it said: DON'T DRINK AND DRIVE. IT'S ONE TEST YOU CAN'T AFFORD TO FAIL.

'Wow,' Jeff thought taking in the message.

Then there was an illustration of a human body with a smoking cigarette as it's head. The caption above read: DON'T BE A BUTT-HEAD.

A man in civilian clothes came into the exam room and closed the door, "You sent for me, Doc?"

"Um, yes. Mr. Wilson thank you for being patient," the doctor began and Jeff didn't like anything that his senses were communicating to him, "My name is doctor Lynbrook and this fine young man is David Thomas. Dave is a HIV and AIDS counselor . . ."

The room began to spin as the doctor continued to speak, his words turning Jeff's world upside down.

". . . if your results had come back negative then there would have been no need for a second test. However, your test results came back positive, Mr. Wilson, so we subsequently proceeded to conduct the second test which confirmed what we learned from the first test. Do you understand what I'm saying to you?"

Jeff wanted to speak but the words were stuck. They just wouldn't' come out. The AIDS counselor intervened,

"Mr. Wilson, I know how you must feel right now, but, you have to believe me, it's not the end of the world. I deal with hundreds of people, maybe thousands who are HIV positive yet they're living full, productive lives . . ."

Jeff couldn't believe this was happening to him. First the murder charge, and now this. He wondered what he did to deserve what was happening to him. He tried to be a good person. He tried his hardest!

"Is there anyone that you want us to contact? It's important that you notify your previous partners, if any, that you've been intimate with. We can do it for you or you can do it on your own."

'Tasia! Oh my God, no, please don't do this to me.'

Jeff must've appeared to be on the verge of a panic attack because David Thomas placed his hands on both of Jeff's shoulders.

"Listen to me . . . " he said trying to get Jeff's attention, "look at me," When Jeff looked into his eyes he continued, "Get yourself together because you're going to get through this, but, you need to be strong. I'm going to sign you up for a support group, we meet once a week and we learn how to take this thing one day at a time. Can I count on you to show up?"

Jeff nodded his head up and down.

"Great! In the meantime the Doc is going to try to find the right combination of medicine to keep you in good shape. There's all kind of options."

When the counselor left, Dr. Lynwood took Jeff's temperature, checked his blood pressure, weighed him and drew blood. He scheduled Jeff to come back for more blood tests and sent him on his way. When the Keyshia Cole replica saw Jeff come from out of the exam room, one look at his face and she knew he had just received bad news. And that was too bad because she really liked him. To just think, she was about ready to take their little meetings to a next level. As Jeff walked out of medical looking like a zombie she warned herself to be more careful. '*Got to be more careful!*'

CHAPTER 33

The new Rick Ross song was playing on the radio and Tasia was putting her own little remix on it.

"Sight seeing . . . I might be in, the Lexus coupe or the new white B.M --"

She and Veronica were in her SC430 driving down Merrick coming from Jamaica Avenue.

Tasia sang in delight, "I use to fight with my moms, Jeff sat us both down now I'm tight with my moms!"

The sad part was that Tasia was oblivious to the mind blowing things that were taking place that would eventually alter her life forever. So, for the time being she was happy, as any sane person would prefer to be.

Jeff had been gone for almost four months, and the lawyer wasn't working as fast as Tasia would have liked so she had decided to take some matters in her own hands.

She began to pump Jeff for information on the sly and she worked with Steve until they learned Chip's full birth name and where his mother lived. Then Tasia went to the 103rd precinct right off of Jamaica Avenue and told them everything she knew. She explained that the blood found at the scene where Green Eyes was killed was in fact the blood of the real murderer. She then gave them Chip's real name and his alias along with the address to his mother's house. The detective she spoke to was kind and he took notes, but, he also said he couldn't make any promises about anything because as far as the District Attorney was concerned they already had the killer in custody.

"Bitch, they can't tell you nothing now. This car is bad!" Ronnie said snapping her fingers to the music.

It was cool outside but the sun was out, and they had the top down on the Lex as they cruised through the streets of Queens. Tasia had on her 'sucka duckers'; a pair of Gucci sunglasses that hugged her face, and she was dressed modestly in a double faced lemon cashmere coat with matching lemon pants and a turtle neck sweater.

"Girl, they couldn't tell me nothing when I was driving my Honda!" Tasia responded giving her girl a high five.

"Hello!" Ronnie said putting a stamp on what Tasia said, then she continued, "Tay, we need to go out tonight. When is the last time we went out? Let's go to the Village Door and listen to some jazz while we have a few drinks, we don't have to stay long."

"Yeah, I guess we can do that. Call Missy and see if she's trying to hang."

"You took the thought right out of my head," Ronnie said reaching for her cell phone.

That's when Mary J. Bilge' song 'Be Without You' came on and Tasia automatically thought about Jeff. Her baby was somewhere locked in a cage and here she was partying like a rock star. Then as quick as the snap of a finger the sympathy was gone and Tasia was mad at Jeff. He didn't have to be locked up! He made the choice to take the blame for a crime he didn't commit, and as a result she was left out in the world by herself.

It was Jeff's fault that she had to sleep alone at night. Come to think about it, she tried to get his ass to stay in the house the night that he got locked up, but, nooooooo, he didn't want to listen.

Tasia mentally threw the book at Jeff in order to justify her going to hang out with her girlfriends. For four months she did nothing but work, and stay at home, and when she wasn't doing that she was busy trying to be there for Jeff in every way possible. Yeah, she deserved a break, and honestly a girls night out was way over due.

CHAPTER 34

Jeff was in his cell stressed out! The pamphlet he read said that one of the symptoms of HIV was a thick white thrush appearing on a person's tongue. Jeff was in the mirror with his tongue out, but he didn't notice anything different about it. He remembered the bout he had with diarrhea, which was also a symptom, but, he couldn't recall ever finding a bruise-like discoloration on his body. Jeff lifted up his shirt and examined his upper body carefully, then he dropped his pants and searched the lower part. It wasn't until Jeff lifted up his testicles that he noticed a bluish purplish mark on his upper thigh.

'*Damn!*' Jeff thought, '*I got it! I got the monster!*'

The monster was one of the terms used to identify AIDS in the hood. They also called it '*the bug*', '*that shit*', '*ninja*', and a variety of other offensive terms.

Up until now Jeff allowed himself a degree of denial, he secretly hoped that there was still a chance that the test results were wrong. But now he remembered the hot and cold sweats, the headaches, and the hardcore bout with diarrhea. Alone these things were nothing, but, together along with the discoloration he just found was enough to seal the deal.

'*Tropical,*' Jeff thought as he tried to figure out how he became infected, '*It had to be Tropical.*'

Jeff remembered the night at the strip club down in V.I.P., he fell victim and he had let Tropical seduce him. They had used a condom, but, when Tropical climbed her heart shaped ass off of him, Jeff saw that the condom had broke. It was all his fault, he never should've gone to the strip club, and he never should've cheated.

Jeff knew he had to tell Tasia and he wondered how his soul mate was going to take the news. He knew she wasn't going to be pleased. On the contrary, he knew this was the kind of news that crushed spirits. It was a life and death matter that could easily break the strongest person down like a fraction.

As Jeff thought about Tasia he now knew he needed to be strong. If not for him, then for her. His mom once told him that you could never measure a person's strength based on the way they held up during the good times . . . a person's strength could only be measured by the way they held up in the face of adversity.

So Jeff came to grips with the fact that his strength was being tested, and the more he thought about it the stronger he became.

'I'm going to get through this,' Jeff thought, *'I'm going to pass the test.'*

The Village Door was a hole in the wall Supper club/ bar on Baisley boulevard right across the street from Rochdale Village. When you walked in through either of the two entrances the bar dominated the right side of the club. On the left side was a raised platform with ten tables lined up in two rows. A giant screen T.V. was sitting at the far end of the two rows of tables and a small platform stage was at the back of the club, this was where the live jazz band was cranking up the tunes. At the front of the club between the two entrances was the juke box. Patrons would feed quarters into the jukebox whenever the band took a break, and the sounds of Kenny G, Anita Baker, and Sade' were among the tunes commonly selected.

Tasia, Missy, and Veronica sat at a table that was against the far left wall drinking Long Island Iced tea and eating platters of fish and chips. The girls were enjoying the music and each other's company, laughing and joking the whole time.

"Girl, I told y'all about my client that just bought the condo near Central Park, right?" Tasia asked feeling good to be out with her girls.

"Yeah, that's the deal you just closed," Missy said.

"Uh huh, but what I didn't tell you was that the brother is fine," Tasia said in a conspiratorial tone.

"Get out of here, Tasia! If you say the nigga is fine then he must be all that and a bag of chips," Ronnie proclaimed.

"I know that's right," Missy added, "because this bitch normally can't see past her Jeff."

"Be quiet and listen . . . ole boy looks like Rakim from Eric B and Rakim, but, he's more muscular. And he's intelligent, this nigga had the nerve to scream on me about dressing like a hooker."

"Get the fuck outta here!" Missy screamed, "That's why your ass been dressing all conservative lately?"

"Don't hate, if it wasn't for Jeff I'd have that fine ass nigga wrapped around my finger. Did I mention how much he spent on that condo? The boy got money. If I was one of these gold diggin' bitches I would've hit the jackpot," Tasia said, the liquor in her system doing most of the talking, "Matter of fact, Jeff better hurry up and bring his ass home because just thinking about Raheem is making my pussy wet."

"Ooooooh, Tasia you better stop!" Ronnie teased.

"His name is Raheem, huh?" Missy asked scheming.

"Y'all know I'm just talking, I wouldn't do nothing crazy, but a bitch do have an itch that needs to be scratched."

Three the hard way fell out laughing. They had a good time at the club and when it was over Tasia was happy she went. After she dropped her girls off she went straight home and crashed. She woke up the next morning to the sound of the phone ringing. It was Jeff.

"Hey baby, what you doing calling this early?" Tasia said looking at the clock. It was eight forty five in the morning and she had a migraine.

"I just wanted to make sure you was still coming up today," He said trying to sound normal.

"Baby, you know I'm coming up there today, why wouldn't I? Is everything okay?"

Jeff paused and Tasia didn't miss it.

"Nah, I just got something to talk to you about."

Tasia was wide awake now.

"So talk about it," she said.

"We'll talk when you get here, " Jeff said standing firm.

"What is it about, your case?"

"Boo, I said we'll talk when you get here."

"Then why you had to say something about it if you know you're not going to tell me, you know I hate when you do that!"

"I love you!" Jeff said in response.

"Yeah whatever."

"What time are you coming?"

"Don't worry about it, you'll see me when I get there."

"Oh it's like that?" Jeff asked.

"No, you know I love you! I'll be there about twelve."

CHAPTER 35

Jeff never quite understood the magnitude of the statement that people sometimes made concerning the calm before the storm. Yet he found himself in the midst of tranquility, the likes of which he'd never experienced before, at a time in his life that could only be described as hurricane season. Jeff was embracing his struggle. He made a conscious decision to accept the challenge.

At first, Jeff's fear was based on the assumption that he didn't have long to live. But the more he pondered, the more he realized that this was the plight of man even without the affliction of a disease.

'Every soul shall taste death,' Jeff thought correctly, *'Nobody is going to live forever.'*

Jeff like millions of others had ignored this reality for most of his life, the only time he thought about death was when somebody died.

"Wilson!" Jeff heard the CO. yell interrupting his chain of thought, "Visit!"

Jeff took a deep breath and exhaled slowly before grabbing his prison I.D. card. He left his cell with his head up, determined to stay strong in the face of adversity.

"Have a good one, son!" Chill said as he pulled a chair

up next to the phone.

"No doubt."

When Jeff made it inside the visiting room he tried his best to maintain a poker face, but, as soon as he saw Tasia the flood gates threatened to burst. All the strength he thought he had was on the lam!

"Baby, what's wrong?" Tasia asked as she took Jeff into her arms.

Jeff just let it all go. He cried like a baby, his shoulders jumping up and down like an old school Chevy fixed with hydraulics.

"It's okay, Jeff, I'm here now." she said in her soothing voice.

Moments later when Jeff was still crying, Tasia was slightly embarrassed because everyone else had already sat down and they were the only ones still standing. Furthermore Tasia was becoming worried, Jeff was like a rock-- what the hell was he crying about?

"You okay now?" she asked, giving Jeff a hint that he needed to get himself together.

Jeff responded by giving her an extra squeeze before he let her go, and he tried to wipe the tears away as he sat down. People were stealing glances in their direction but Jeff had more important things to think about, he couldn't worry about the small things.

"I love you," Tasia said matter of factly, as if Jeff may have forgotten. It was intended to give Jeff strength but it almost succeeded in opening back up the flood gates.

"I love you too," Jeff managed to get out.

Tasia was baffled. She wondered if Jeff had spoken to

the lawyer and received some bad news or something.

"You spoke to your lawyer?" she asked after a bit, she was losing her patience.

Jeff shook his head to say no. His right hand was balled into a fist and he repeatedly banged it softly against his head.

"You want to talk about it?" Tasia asked.

Jeff nodded his head to say yes.

"O.K." Tasia said as if she was giving him permission.

After a moment, Jeff asked her: "You know I love you, right?"

Tasia didn't really feel like playing this game, but, she went along anyway, "Of course. I love you too."

"And, you know I would die for you, you're my soul mate. I probably love you more than I love myself."

"Okay."

"And I feel I should be able to tell you anything---"

"And you can."

"And it should never come between what we have, our bond."

"Get to the point," Tasia finally said. She needed Jeff to come clean because she hated the beat around the bush game, and she was starting to get upset.

"Boo, I don't want you to hate me--"

"You sound stupid, Jeff, you know I'm not going to hate you. Just tell me what the hell is going on."

Jeff shook his head back and forth. He knew he couldn't get around what needed to be done so he just went ahead and dropped the first dose of napalm.

"I cheated on you."

It took about five seconds for Tasia to process what Jeff

had said and she sat across from him with her mouth open in disbelief.

"You did what?"

"I cheated--"

"I heard what the fuck you said!" Tasia damn near screamed.

They remained in silence for a bit with Tasia shooting daggers across the table at Jeff.

"You know what, you're a weak mother fucker. Do you know how many niggaz try to talk to me in the course of a day? Can you imagine Jeff? You've been locked up for four months and my dumb ass been holding you down, and now you're telling me that your *It's me and you against the world, Boo'* ass cheated on me? You can't be serious, and if this is your idea of a joke, it's not funny!"

"It was only one time--"

"What? Jeff don't make me come across this table, you need to quit while you're ahead. I'm not trying to hear that lame shit. You come out here with all that crying, I bet you wasn't crying when you was fucking cheating! What you think you're the only one who likes to fuck, Jeff? Huh? I like to get my pussy licked! But I never disrespected you or myself by cheating! I wish I would give a motherfucker some pussy when I'm already involved in a relationship, that would make the relationship meaningless. That's some weak shit and you played yourself."

Jeff let Tasia vent. Nothing was going the way it was suppose to and he knew that he still needed to tell her about the other thing. He needed to persuade her to get tested and he needed her to continue to be by his side.

"What's her name?"

The question caught Jeff by surprise.

"Who?"

"Don't play stupid with me, what's the bitch's name that you cheated with?"

Jeff was getting frustrated now.

"That's not even important, Tasia," he said trying to regain some control over the situation.

"Nigga, if you don't tell me that bitch's name I will get up and leave! Now go 'head and try me…"

Poor Jeff!

"Her name is Tropical," Jeff said in defeat.

Tasia crunched up her face, "Tropical? What the fuck is that, a stripper?"

"Tasia," Jeff pleaded, looking for a break, "This is already hard enough as it is, and you have a right to be upset but, I still didn't tell you what I need to tell you."

"You still didn't tell me what you need to tell me? Jeff *please!* What else could you possibly have to tell me? You have to admit, you cheating on me is going to be a hard act to follow," Tasia said turning sideways in her chair so she wasn't facing Jeff. She didn't even want to look at him.

Jeff was sad, but, he had to push forward. Without warning he spit it out, "Baby . . . I'm HIV positive."

Tasia's body went rigid!

'I know he didn't say what I think he just said. Lord please don't do this to me . . . not now, not like this.'

Tasia turned in her seat and in a calm manner she asked, "What did you just say, Jeff, I don't think I heard you correctly."

At that point Jeff sat there wishing he was never born. Whoever said that life was easy obviously never walked a mile in his shoes.

"Repeat what you said . . . I said I didn't' hear you," Tasia reiterated in that same calm tone.

"I'm HIV positive."

Tasia nodded her head up and down, "That's what I thought you said."
And Tasia came across the table! She was swinging wildly, scratching Jeff's face and clawing at his eyes.

"I hate you!" Tasia screamed, "I hope you die tonight!"

Jeff was trying to subdue her but he couldn't do it alone. C.O. Taylor and another C.O. made their way over in record breaking time and pried Tasia off of Jeff.

"You gave me that shit! You may as well had put a gun to my head and pulled the trigger!" Tasia screamed as the officers pulled her away.

"I hate you! Word to Day-day I hate you!"

Jeff just stood there in defeat. Tasia's words would resonate in his head for the rest of his days. Whatever was left of his life he knew he would be hard pressed trying to erase those words . . . and those were the last words Tasia ever said to Jeff.

CHAPTER 36

Betrayal! Tasia felt as if she'd been betrayed by one of the few people on the planet that she truly trusted. She couldn't even remember how she made it home from Rikers Island after the visit, that's how torn apart she was. One thing she was certain of, if Jeff was HIV positive, then so was she.

Tasia cried, she threw things, she screamed and cursed at the top of her lungs, and she collapsed on the cold floor out of sheer defeat.

Tasia forwarded all incoming calls on her cell phone to her voice mail. This was done after she called her job and explained to Mr. Armstrong that she needed to take at least two weeks off. His dumb ass expressed concern but there was really nothing he could do. Tasia's home became her personal prison. She wouldn't leave the house for nothing.

Missy and Veronica were worried about their friend because she wasn't answering her phone or returning their calls. Then when they came by the house, both Tasia's car and Jeff's truck were in the driveway, yet no one was answering the door.

"Leave me the fuck alone!" Tasia screamed at the empty room whenever someone attempted to violate her isolated space.

She was sitting on the kitchen floor with her legs pulled close to her chest, drinking vodka straight from the bottle. She had bags under her eyes from a lack of sleep, she was barely eating, and she was neglecting her hygiene. At one point Tasia even contemplated suicide.

There was a mail slot in Tasia's front door, and after the third day of being holed up, the letters from Jeff began pouring in. Small envelopes, standard envelopes, manila envelopes, all thick and stuffed with literature and communication from Jeff were basically ignored and most items went straight in the trash.

Tasia in her drunken state would get creative in expressing herself.

"Fuck you, Jeff, fuck you . . . I hope your mother fucking ass die-- fuck you, Jeff, fuck you . . . our relationship was one big lie!"

Tasia's heart grew cold over night, she was a good girl gone bad. She tried to escape reality by staying drunk, but, the stash she kept in the house for when she had company was running low. She was consuming large amounts of alcohol on a daily basis, most times drinking until she passed out. She would awake in different rooms of the house, sometimes on the floor, and not remember how she got there. However, Tasia always remembered who was to blame for her woes.

"God, please, strike his dog ass down!" she would cry at the drop of a dime, "I swear on my baby brother I hope you die tonight Jeff, that's word to Day-day."

After Tasia was missing in action for over three weeks, Missy and Ronnie got on some *who's that peeking in my window* shit. After ringing the door bell and banging on the door they began walking around the house looking in windows. The window to Tasia's bedroom was too high to see in so Ronnie put her hands together and gave Missy a boost so she could look inside. Once Missy got her balance she cupped her hands to the window and surveyed the room.

"Oh shit! There that bitch go right there," Missy said banging on the window, "Tasia! Come open the door!"

Tasia was sitting on her bed looking at Missy's crazy ass trying to keep her balance.

"Tasia, come to the door!"

"I heard you, shit!" Tasia yelled.

Tasia went and opened the door and then went and grabbed the bottle of E&J she found stashed in the hallway closet. When she walked back into the living room her two best friends were standing there with their mouths open as they looked around. Empty liquor bottles littered the floor, ripped up pictures and broken frames were all over the place, the fish in the fish tank were all dead . . . the house was out of order!

"What the fuck?" Missy started in disbelief, "Tasia what happened in here?"

Tasia was sitting on the couch about to drink E&J from the bottle but Ronnie snatched it away from her. Ronnie was on the verge of tears.

"Shit, if you wanted some all you had to do was ask, you don't have to be snatching nothing from nobody," Tasia said looking at Ronnie with contempt.

"Tasia did you lose your mind? Look at you!" Missy said wondering how Tasia allowed herself to fall this far.

Tasia just sucked her teeth without responding. Ronnie was too shocked to speak but Missy had questions.

"Girl, no disrespect but, I know you're not tripping over no nigga? Jeff is cool but, aint NO nigga in the world worth what you're putting yourself through. If the shoe was on the other foot I know aint *no* nigga going to stress himself to death over a bitch, so you may as well get your shit together!"

"Is that what this is about, Tasia?" Ronnie asked as if she was going to lose control and start crying at any second.

"Bitch, what else you think it's about?" Missy asked sarcastically, "They locked up her man for murder, and now her dumb ass is in here trying to kill herself."

Tasia was looking at Missy with pure hatred in her eyes. "Jeff is going to beat them charges, Tasia, you just wait and see," Ronnie said with conviction.

"And if he don't, then that's on him," Missy added harshly.

"Don't say that Missy, that's not right," Ronnie argued.

"Bitch, fuck that, I think that nigga was fucking Charlene anyway I just didn't want to say nothing because this bitch was acting like she was all in love and shit."

Ronnie couldn't believe Missy was standing there flipping on Jeff like that.

"Yeah that's right, and the only reason I'm saying something now is because I'm not about to let you torture yourself over a nigga that aint shit. You up in here acting like you done bumped your head. I should've said something before, but, as long as you was happy, I was cool. But now you know, Niggaz aint shit! They're dogs, every last one of them."

Tasia was listening closely to everything that Missy said. When Missy was finished with her tirade, Tasia wore a wicked smile on her face.

"Bitch, you dead right. I don't know what the fuck I was thinking about," She said looking from Missy to Ronnie, "Yall help me clean this raggedy ass house up so I can get myself together."

Ronnie gave Tasia a big hug and Missy gave them both a high five. Missy had just created a monster and she wasn't even aware of it.

Tasia felt that since niggaz wasn't shit, and all men were dogs, then she was going to give *'that package'* to as many of their dog asses as she could.

'They can blame Jeff for this shit I'm about to unleash on their asses!'

CHAPTER 37

The HIV/AIDS support group session was held in the school area of C-74. When Jeff entered the classroom where the session was taking place, a group consisting of eight people was sitting in a circle already engaged in discussion. When David Thomas, the HIV/AIDS awareness counselor noticed Jeff standing in the doorway, he beckoned him over and instructed the group to spread their chairs out to make room. Someone quickly grabbed a chair and added it to the circle.

As Jeff took a seat, Dave took the initiative and introduced him to the rest of the group.

"Gentlemen, I want you to meet Jeff! Jeff volunteered to sit with us this week and I ask that you make him feel welcomed. Who knows, he may even return next week. Jeff, this is an open session, if you want to share anything, feel free. If you prefer to listen, that's okay too. However, we just have one rule, and that's that you respect whoever has the floor."

That didn't sound too hard. Jeff sat there and listened to the struggles that some of the guys experienced as a result of being HIV positive. One guy said that his mother accused him of being gay, and disowned him for having what she called *'The gay people disease'*. Jeff was appalled that a mother could be so cruel to her child and he silently wondered how his own mother would react to the news when he told her.

A slim dark complexioned guy had his hand in the air, and Dave gave him the green light to address the group.

"Yeah fellas, most of you already know me but for those of you who don't, my name is Shane. Although I'm not HIV positive, it's definitely my goal to learn as much as possible about HIV and AIDS so I can educate my friends and family. My aunt Luisa died from AIDS, and I remember one time when she was sick and we all went to visit her in the hospital. We had to put masks over our faces before going into her room but my cousins boyfriend was acting like he didn't' want to put the mask on. He thought he was being loyal to my aunt by refusing to put on a mask in order to be around her, but he was really ignorant. The doctor had to explain to him, the doctor said: "Listen, the mask isn't for your protection, it's for hers. Any germs that you carry, even a common cold, can pose a threat to her weakened immune system."

Thankfully my cousin's boyfriend put the mask on after that, but, that's just one example why I want to learn as much as I can about this disease. People in general are ignorant and knowledge is power."

Throughout the session Jeff learned a great deal. A few times he heard people express the importance of maintaining a high T-cell count and Jeff made a mental note to learn more about that. For the most part he felt comfortable with the group, and he decided even before the session was over that he would attend again. He also vowed to send a copy of all the information he received to Tasia. He hoped that she was smart enough to go and get tested, and he prayed that she wasn't infected, but, it was the not knowing that was killing him.

CHAPTER 38

Missy and Ronnie escorted Tasia to the beauty parlor on 149th Street and Jamaica avenue, and Tasia felt like the meanest bitch alive after receiving a fresh perm. Tasia was in baller catcher mode, she had on an Escru waist tied camisole by Carolina Herrera and some Apple Bottom jeans that had her ass looking good enough to eat.

Three the hard way was just leaving the nail salon when a grey S550 Mercedes Benz stopped in the middle of the street and the passenger side window glided down effortlessly.

"Damn Ronnie, that's how you doing it?" the driver asked as he appraised the three beautiful sisters.

Ronnie was smiling from ear to ear, "Boy, I need to be doing it like you, you haven't been home a hot ninety days and you're already pushing the new S-class."

"Girl, who's that?" Missy asked punching Ronnie's arm.

"That's Ivan from Baisley, he just came home from the Feds."

"I'm saying though," Ivan was saying as cars honked their horns behind him trying to get him to move his car out of the middle of the street, "Your home girl is killin' 'em in them Apple Bottom jeans, that ass is in a class by itself."

Tasia turned around and locked her legs back, giving

Ivan a hardcore back shot. She looked over her shoulder and smiled at the expression on his face.

"It doesn't make sense just looking at it if you're not trying to do nothing with it," she said as she boldly slapped her ass.

Both Missy and Ronnie were standing there with their mouths open in shock from Tasia's behavior.

"Oh, it's like that?" Ivan asked continuing to hold up traffic.

"It's however you want it to be!" Tasia shot back.

"Damn Boo, you a bad mutha fucka, but if you giving it away like that you might have that shit! I came too far to get caught like that -- I'm good! But yall ladies have a nice day anyway."

While Ivan was driving off, Tasia was cursing his ass out. Now she *really* couldn't wait to burn a nigga's ass up.

As the trio started walking back toward Jamaica Avenue a guy with long dreadlocks caught a whiff of the perfume Tasia had on.

"Excuse me, beautiful lady . . . " he said grabbing Tasia by the hand which was usually a no-no, "Ya smell marvelous, ya hear? Me just wan' know ya name?" he continued smoothly in his heavy west indian accent.

Tasia was still pissed off over the way Ivan had treated her, but, she remained focused on her mission. Instinctively she thought of the person partially to blame for her predicament, then without giving it much thought the words just danced off of her tongue like music, "Tropical. My name is Tropical."

Missy and Ronnie just stared at each other with baffled expressions on their faces. They didn't know who the hell this imposter was, but they concluded that it damn sure wasn't Tasia!

They watched their friend exchange phone numbers with the rude boy and then they continued on without comment. When they made it back to the spot where Tasia's Lexus was parked, Missy could no longer control herself.

"Bitch, I just got one question," she said as Tasia put her key in the ignition, "Who the fuck is Tropical?"

CHAPTER 39

Shakim was young, black, and on his way to being rich, and he was loving every minute of it. The recession was a blessing in disguise the way Sha saw it, because he wasn't a bit concerned with all of the people losing their homes due to foreclosures. To Sha, foreclosures meant opportunity. Shit, his uncle Raheem was able to cop a condo on Central Park West for less than five million dollars, a condo that normally would've sold for about eight or nine million easily. That's what Sha thought the real estate game was all about; buying low and selling high. And the best time to buy low was at times when the market was in trouble, if only you could weather the storm. Because the storm never lasted forever, and the value of real estate would always sky-rocket after the hard times. That was Shakim's way of thinking.

Now it was a little after one in the morning and Sha was in the Range hauling ass down Guy R. Brewer boulevard. He was on his way to The Scene, a small club across the street from junior high school 72 in Rochdale Village. The club actually changed its name a dozen times but to Shakim it would always be known as The Scene.

As Shakim drove past Linden boulevard he smiled as he thought about Shelly, he knew her dusty ass was probably standing under the truss trying to hustle up some change. A few nights before, Sha had rolled up on the little strip and beeped his horn at Shelly while she was at a car talking to a potential trick. Knowing that Sha was "sure money" Shelly had dismissed the guy in the car and came walking toward the black Range Rover. As soon as she got to the window on the passenger side of the SUV Shakim pulled off leaving Shelly standing there with the jackass look. In the rearview mirror he saw her giving him the finger and she looked mad as hell.

Now as Sha approached the truss he could see Shelly and a few other crack heads standing out there trying to do their thing. There was a big puddle of water near the curb from when it rained, and as much as Sha hated to dirty up the Range, he couldn't resist swooping over and driving right through that puddle of water and splashing the shit out of Shelly and her co-workers.

Shakim got a good laugh out of that and his heartless ass felt no remorse.

'All them bitches need now is some soap and they'd be straight,' he thought as he drove pass Baisley Projects. His thoughts momentarily went to Black Nicole. He was tempted to make a booty call and scoop her little ass up, but, he decided to wait and see what was popping at the Scene. If he couldn't catch something proper then he would settle for Blackie.

When Shakim arrived at the club, it appeared to be packed to capacity judging from all the cars in the vicinity. There were whips all up on the sidewalk and then you had the ones that were double parked blocking mother fuckers in. Shakim found a spot to double park that was right near the club's exit. He jumped out the Range and it seemed like all eyes were on him. Baby boy thought he was a playboy for real and he was playing his part to a tee.

"Ayo! Sha!" someone called from the front of the club.

Sha didn't catch the voice, but, upon closer inspection he recognized Gabe and another dude that he didn't know, leaning against Steve's Dodge Charger.

"What up, Gabe... where's Steve at?" Shakim said as he approached Gabe and gave him dap.

"He's up in there getting his groove on." Gabe said watching the surroundings.

"Why you ain't up in there?" Sha asked.

"Man, I'm tryna catch a vic," Gabe said seriously, "Before the night is over I'm tryna rob me a mutha fucka."

Shakim was checking out a bad bitch in a super short mini-dress that damn near stumbled out of the club's exit. She was obviously drunk and she almost fell down the stairs if homeboy that was with her didn't grab her arm. Ole boy had on an eye catching chain, and a sliver of bling poked out from his sleeve.

Shakim glanced at Gabe and saw the gleam in his eyes.

"True story, Gabe . . . " Sha said in an effort to prevent the inevitable, "That shit aint even worth it. Go 'head and take half this stack and leave that shit alone."

Shakim pulled out a brick of money and broke bread with the little homie.

Gabe had to smile, "You got that, Fam, you just gave that nigga a pass." He put the money that Sha handed him in his pocket and decided to chill until Sha left.

Shakim was a shiesty dude for real, he didn't care if Gabe robbed the pope, he just didn't want to be around when it happened. With his luck, they would mess around and make him a co-defendant in the robbery just because he was there kicking it with Gabe.

Sha was looking at the entrance of the club and almost had to do a double take when he saw a familiar face in the midst of a group of bad ass bitches.

'Oh shit! Tasia!' Sha thought as he automatically got on some Hugh Hefner shit.

"Ayo Gabe, Imma get up with you, ya heard? Yall stay out of trouble, I'm about to try to bag one of these bitches."

"Do you, Fam!" Gabe responded happy to be rid of ole boy.

As Shakim approached the group of women, they were laughing and carrying on in their own little world. Tasia had on a transparent mesh jump-suit that hugged every curve on her body, and Sha was instantly aroused. He licked his lips and called her name.

Tasia paused and looked at him and Sha could tell that she'd been drinking.

"What's up Tasia, Could I talk to you for a minute?" Sha asked looking at her as if he wanted to eat her alive.

"Who's Tasia?" She retorted as if she was amused.

That threw Sha for a loop, but, he was in mack mode so he bounced right back.

"Oh, my bad, Sweetness, you look like a super model I know, she doubles as a real estate agent. Anyway, what's your name?

Tasia giggled, *'Isn't he the witty one,'* she thought as Shakim molested her with his eyes.

"My name is Tropical."

'*Damn, I can't believe by luck!*' Sha thought, '*This bitch is tryna fuck, it's written all over her face!*'

"Okay Tropical, how about if we lose your friends and jet to this after party?"

"After party, huh?" Tasia smiled with a knowing look, "If I didn't know any better, I'd say you was trying to get me alone so you could take advantage of me and get you some of this killer pussy."

'*Killer pussy, get it?*' Tasia thought sarcastically.

"And if that was my plan?" Sha asked testing the water.

"I'd say be a man and say what the fuck is on your mind. Little boys waste precious time beating around the bush."

Tasia caught Shakim off guard again with the tone of her voice along with the content of what was said. And again he shook that shit off.

"My bad, and you are absolutely right. Let's get the fuck outta here and go get us a room," Sha spit like a cold blooded pimp.

"Okay," Tasia said with a smirk.

When they got to the Range, Sha opened the passenger door for Tasia.

'*I'm a bad mutha fucka,*' he thought as he strolled around to the drivers side, '*Only if my uncle could see me now.*

Tasia wore a mischievous grin as she watched his dumb ass trying to be cool.

'*Let's see how cool this nigga looks in a casket,*' she thought with hatred flowing through her veins, '*I'm a bad bitch . . . Only if Jeff could see me now!*'

CHAPTER 40

Tasia and Shakim went straight to the Executive Motor Inn on the south conduit. It was approximately 2:30 am when they made it to a room and they wasted no time getting busy with some serious fucking. Tasia noted with disgust that Sha hadn't even attempted to wear a condom. It was no wonder HIV and AIDS posed such an eminent threat to communities throughout the world.

The guy with the dreadlocks that Tasia had met when she went to get her nails and hair done was no different. He didn't know Tasia from a can of paint, yet his desire to attain maximum enjoyment by penetrating her without protection over-rode basic common sense. Tasia wondered how she ever allowed herself to even trust Jeff the way she did when she knew first hand how weak men were when it came to pussy. She had played herself and now she was paying for it big time, but, she was determined not to be the only one who paid.

Tasia and Sha went at it like rabbits until a little after four in the morning, and although ole girl was on a mission, she made sure she enjoyed herself by getting a nut or two.

After being deprived for so long because Jeff was in jail, Tasia was happy to have a healthy supply of dick back in her life. Babygirl was going out with a bang!

After the heart pounding sex she had with Sha, Tasia was able to get a full four hours of sleep. She woke up to the sound of Sha snoring lightly, and a quick glance at the clock on the night stand told her it was almost twenty after eight.

Tasia slipped out of bed feeling no remorse. She showered and got dressed quietly before tip toeing her ass right out of the hotel room. She called a cab from the hotel lobby and was dropped off by her car which was across the street from the club where she left it.

After driving home and changing her clothes, Tasia was ready to go back to work. She couldn't wait to see her boss, Mr. Armstrong, a married man who couldn't keep his dick in his pants.

'I got something for his no good, weak ass,' Tasia thought as she drove to Colossal Realty, *'His dog ass wants to cheat on his wife, well, he might just have to pay with his life. He better ask somebody! Big Tay got that killer pussy!'*

Tasia laughed at her own wit, but, on the inside she was crying. Babygirl was hurting so bad that she wanted the whole world the feel her pain.

CHAPTER 41

Steve, Kaymel, Doonie, and another little homie name Tattoo were on Jamaica Avenue dropping stacks as they ventured on a spur of the moment shopping spree. Kaymel was taking the entire crew to Atlantic City for the weekend, and whenever they stepped out together as a team he wanted everybody to shine.

Kaymel was an up and coming boss and he was dying to take his game to another level. The way he planned to achieve this goal was by having a top of the line team of goblins. If he was driving, he wanted his niggaz to be driving . . . if he was wearing exclusive jewelry, he wanted his niggaz to be rocking some exclusive jewelry. . . and if Kaymel was stacking that paper, it was only right that his team was right there stacking that paper with him.

So now Kaymel was splurging on a trip to A.C. and he wanted his niggaz to represent to the fullest.

"Stunt 101 my niggaz, let's show these 10 karat gold wearing ass niggaz how the big boys do it!" Kaymel hollered after copping a platinum bracelet that was flooded out with diamonds and rubies.

"Damn son, you killing 'em with that joint right there," Steve said giving Kaymel the stamp of approval.

"Keep the heckler close," Tattoo sung looking at the

bling and remembering a Jigga verse, "You know them smokers will test ya."

Kaymel looked at Tattoo and smiled, "No bullshit, this joint right here is a stick up kid's dream, but that's what the fuck I got you for. Let a nigga jump out there, he gonna think you work at Mc Donalds when he see that Big Mac you toting!"

The team and a couple of shoppers in hearing distance busted out laughing.

When they left the jewelry store, they began walking down the brick road on 165th Street. Everybody had their hands full with bags and was ready to head back to the truck, but, Steve spotted some crushed linen outfits that were off the chain in a new store called The Gentlemen's Closet.

"Hold up yall," Steve said looking at the set up in the window, "Kaymel, run inside with me real quick!"

"Man, we already got too much shit. We gonna have a hard time getting the shit we already got in the truck, you wildin' son," Kaymel responded looking at Steve as if he had to be kidding.

"Come on and hold me down my nigga," Steve said not waiting for a response.

"I'll hold some of this shit in my lap if I have to, I aint worried about that."

Kaymel sucked his teeth and put his bags down near Doonie and Tattoo, "This nigga! We'll be right back yall, keep an eye on the bags."

Five months had already gone by since that fateful night

when Chip had killed Green Eyes. Chip had managed to escape the law, but, on that night when the bullets began to fly, Chip didn't manage to escape the bullet that had his name on it. The bullet actually only grazed his shoulder, but by the time Chip made it home he had lost a lot of blood. When Felicia saw her son come into the house covered in blood, she began to panic and was about to call an ambulance.

"No!" Chip yelled through clinched teeth, "just help me try to stop the bleeding."

Chip's mom was confused at first, but then Chip explained to her that someone had been killed. If he went to a hospital, he told his mom, she would probably lose him for the next twenty-five years.

Felicia didn't like it, but, the prospect of losing her son for such a long period of time was unthinkable, so she called her friend Gloria who was a registered nurse. Gloria came and attended to Chip as best she could, cleaning the wound and dressing it up and also providing an ample amount of pain killers.

Chip laid low for months, he didn't leave the house for nothing. He heard about Jeff being locked up and he felt bad about it, but turning himself in wasn't an option.

If there was any other way that he could help Jeff then he would, but he wasn't going to jail for nobody.

Now five months later, Chip's shoulder had healed and as far as he was concerned the heat had died down. He kept his ear to the street through his mother and his cousin Jimmy. Jimmy was the one that told him about some dudes from Forty projects that was suppose to be looking for him.

"Yeah, whatever," Chip had said when Jimmy first told him, "Seek and they shall find! They better learn a lesson from what happened to their mutha fuckin' man, I aint playing with these niggaz!"

And Chip was dead serious. When he finally came out of his hole, ole boy was armed and dangerous. The first thing he did was drive to Jamaica Avenue so he could get a few new outfits. He had his mom's Nissan Altima, and after smoking a blunt to the head and listening to that Murda Incorporated song by DMX, Jay-Z, and Ja-Rule,

Chip was ready for whatever. He was singing Jay's verse in his head as he walked down the brick road on 165th Street.

'I dip, squat, and post up, with the toast up, I bring beef to a closure . . .'

While Doonie and Tattoo waited for Steve and Kaymel to come out of the store, Tattoo was shooting his game at almost every chick that walked by while Doonie was busy talking on his cell phone.

Doonie was just ending his call when he saw a face coming toward him that made his eyes wide like saucers.

The element of surprise had Doonie like a deer caught in headlights, but, Chip not only expected danger -- he was looking for it!

As Doonie called Tattoo's name to put him on point, Chip was reaching for the chrome 9mm Taurus that he had tucked in his waist.

Doonie nor Tattoo never had a chance! Chip opened fire with no regard for the innocent people around, yet, at such close range it was almost impossible for him to miss his intended targets. He burned Doonie and Tattoo up, and as people screamed, ducked, and ran for cover, Chip spun around and tried to get low.

Unfortunately for Chip, the boys in blue lived on the Avenue! Their precinct was just a block away. If Chip was on a football field he wouldn't have even made a first down. Cops came from everywhere like roaches in the projects when the lights come on. An ambitious rookie cop tackled Chip from his blind side.

By the time Steve and Kaymel peeked out of the store, Doonie and Tattoo were already dead and Chip was being led away in handcuffs.

CHAPTER 42

"Grandma, this macaroni and cheese is off the chain," Shakim said, talking with his mouth full.

"Thank you, baby, you want some more?" the older woman asked passing the baked macaroni and cheese across the table, "And what I tell you about talking with your mouth full?"

"My bad, it's just that this food is so good," Sha responded as he piled more food onto his plate.

The kitchen table was looking like soul food Sunday at Big Mama's house! There was fried chicken, roast beef, mashed potatoes, candied yams, rice, collard greens with smoked turkey neck, macaroni and cheese, stuffing, gravy, and mouth watering sweet potatoe pie.

"Ma, you still didn't tell your grandson the big news. Let me find out you're trying to pull a Houdini move," Raheem said smiling at his mother, which was Shakim's grandmother.

Shakim was stuffing his face but he looked from his uncle to his grandmother trying to figure out what Raheem was talking about.

"Boy, hush, I'm not trying to pull anything. I was just waiting for the right time."

"Right time for what, grandma?"

"Well," she said wiping her hands on a napkin and

smiling nervously, "I've . . . *we've* decided to leave New York. You know I always wanted a nice house in Florida."

"Grandma, you can't leave New York! Tell her Raheem, we don't even know nobody in Florida."

Shakim's grandmother was the closest thing he had to an actual mother, and he loved her more than anyone else in the world.

"Yeah, I can leave New York, baby, grandma is grown. And you're right, we don't know anybody in Florida, another reason I'm eager to go. There comes a time when you have to spread your wings, baby. Spread your wings and soar."

"Man, grandma, you just messed up my whole night. You know I can't function without you . . . what part of Florida are you talking about moving to?"

"We're talking about moving to Jacksonville," grandma said looking at Sha carefully.

He finally caught on.

"You keep saying we, don't tell me that you talked my mother into moving down there and starting over."

"No, although I wish that were the case," she responded sadly before dropping the bomb, "I'm talking about your uncle Raheem." Shakim's mouth dropped wide open when that message reached his brain.

"What?" he yelled loudly.

"Boy hush all that noise," grandma said waving at Sha for emphasis, "Now you know you're welcome to join us, Sha. Raheem and I had a long talk and we both would hate for you to stay in New York. There's nothing here but trouble. But you're grown Shakim, the final decision is yours."

Shakim was looking at his uncle as if he wanted to hear his wisdom.

"Sha, we're keeping the condo near Central Park so we can come visit whenever we want, but, everything else is either going to be rented out or it's going on the market. I don't know about you but I'm trying to be close to my mama," Raheem said sincerely.

"Me too!" Sha yelled.

"So it's settled then, you're coming with us," Raheem said.

Shakim smiled, but, he was kind of sad because New York was the only home he knew.

"Yeah, it's settled . . . I'm going," he said in defeat.

Sha's grandmother came around the table and gave her grandson a big hug and a kiss on the cheek.

"I love you, baby!" she cried.

"I love you, too, grandma."

Tasia and Missy were in the Lexus flying down Sunrise Highway with the top down bumping Snoop Dogg's 'Doggy Style' CD. Tasia had been an emotional wreck lately, but when she listened to songs where men degraded women she almost felt as if she could justify what she was doing. Almost. She especially felt justified when she listened to Dr. Dre's song on The Chronic CD; Bitches Aint Shit (but hoes and tricks!). That song became Tasia's anthem as she reversed it and treated niggaz as if they were weak and useless.

Tasia had sex with so many guys in the last month that she

couldn't even count them when she tried. Every last one of them had unprotected sex with her, no questions asked except maybe, "Who's pussy is this?" And that was asked during intercourse, not before.

A young cat name Booyah actually surprised Tasia. He was the one out of all of her lovers who insisted on wearing protection. Tasia simply told him that condoms irritated her coochie. Booyah tried to push the issue but Tasia made her position clear—either go raw or don't go at all. Ultimately, Booyah jumped in the pool butt ass naked, raw dawg, just like everybody else.

But lately, Tasia had been second guessing herself. She knew what she was doing was wrong, but, her heart was too cold to stop. She still blamed Jeff, in her mind it was all his fault.

Tasia made a right turn on Guy R. Brewer boulevard. She had to drop Missy's nosey ass off and then she was trying to line up some dick for the night.

As they pulled up to a red light right before they got to Rochdale, one of Tasia's favorite songs came on.

'This is for the Gee's, and this is for the hustlers, this is for the hustlers, now back to the Gee's' .

They pulled off and floated down the boulevard with that gangsta ass shit banging from the system. The next time they got caught at a light was at Foch boulevard. Niggaz from Baisley projects was posted up on the corner and Tasia started flirting as she switched the words up to Snoop's verse.

"How many niggaz in your mother fucking group, wanna take a ride in my mother fucking coupe - - -"

"Bitch, the light is green!" Missy said with her hating ass, but the niggaz on the corner were already throwing their hands in the air trying to get chose.

Tasia winked her eye at their dog asses before driving off.

"You done turned into little miss whore, huh?" Missy asked with a smirk on her face.

"Let me hurry up and drop your ass off, how about that?" Tasia shot back.

After she dropped Missy off, Tasia was about to drive back through Baisley to see what she could catch when a car behind her flashed high beams on and off to get her attention. Tasia pulled over to see who it was. She didn't recognize the bald headed dude approaching from the driver's side until he was right in front of her.

"Oh my goodness, Steve, you're rocking the shiny bald head I didn't even recognize you."

Steve gave a perfunctory smile, but, Tasia could tell he was sad about something.

"Yeah, I cut my hair off after my two little mans and them got killed. I know you heard about that, right?"

"No, I didn't know about that," Tasia responded.

"Yeah, that sucker ass nigga Chip struck again—"

"Ohhh!" Tasia said covering her mouth, "Them two guys that Chip killed on Jamaica Avenue -- those were your friends? I'm so sorry, Steve, poor baby. I was wondering why you were looking all down. That happened about a week ago, right?"

"It's been ten days, but, real talk, I'm cool. And you know I didn't pull you over to talk about that, I was just trying to see how you're doing," Steve said catching a glance of Tasia's short ass skirt riding up those thick thighs.

Tasia didn't miss none of that.

"Shit, I could be better, but, for now I'm still alive so I guess that's a plus," Tasia said and then continued, "What about you? I see you peeking like you see something you want?"

"You caught that, huh?--You know what they say, a person always want what they can't have," Steve shot.

"What makes you think you can't have it?" Tasia asked.

"See, now you're starting to get my dick hard."

"Well let's do something about that."

Steve nodded his head up and down in agreement.

"I got a room at the Holiday Inn near La Guardia Airport . . . if you're serious about doing something with this standard seven then follow me."

"Standard seven?" Tasia asked confused.

"Yep," Steve responded as a smile appeared on his face, "A standard seven inches, that's all the kid is working with, I hope that's alright."

"Boy, you are too much. Get your butt in the car and lead the way,"

She didn't have to tell Steve twice.

Shakim knew he was going to miss New York like crazy, but, he couldn't imagine not being around the only family he knew. He thanked God for blessing him with people who loved him unconditionally.

The truth was, Shakim knew he was a dirty dude. He just couldn't help it! He remembered when he was little, whenever someone would come by the house and they wanted some water to drink, Sha would get it from the toilet. That was some foul shit, but that was just how Sha got down. And deep in his heart he felt bad about the cruddy moves he made.

It was after midnight and although gas prices were

through the roof, Sha was just driving around pondering about life. His grandmother and Raheem said they were going to start moving their things down to Florida in less than forty five days so Sha needed to get his affairs in order.

For some reason, Sha's mind drifted to Shelly. What he did to her was wrong, even if she was the one who burned him. Her son, Buddy, would have it a hundred times worse because of what Sha did. He consciously and diabolically got her hooked on crack!

Without giving it much thought Shakim started driving toward the truss on Guy R. Brewer boulevard near 116th Avenue. When he pulled on the scene he was happy to see that Shelly was out there. He sat in the Range Rover waiting for ole girl to notice him and come over but Shelly was avoiding him.

"Oh now she wanna act like she's mad at me," Sha said to himself before tapping the horn to get her attention.

Shelly stood across the street looking in his direction but she was planted where she stood like a tree.

Shakim put his hands together in a begging motion like he use to do whenever he wanted something bad, and Shelly reluctantly began to cross the street. She was walking slowly as if she expected Sha to pull off at any second.

Instead of going around to the passenger side, Shelly came straight to the driver's side window. When she was close enough Sha was able to get a whiff of the foul odor coming from her body.

"Don't be mad at me," Sha said with a grin, but, he was trying to be sincere.

Shelly just stared at him wondering what she did that was so bad to make him do her the way he did. Her whole life went down hill because of Sha and here he was all up in her face smiling.

"I'm sorry, Shelly, stop looking at me like that," he said.

Sha was happy that he apologized to her, but, as she just stood there not saying anything, Shakim's mind switched gears. He started thinking about getting his dick sucked.

"Shit, if you don't want to use your mouth to talk I got something else you can do with it, AND you can make yourself $20," Sha said licking his lips.

When he saw the fire that leaped into Shelly's eyes he had to laugh. Ole girl was really upset, and the truth was that she had every right to be.

As Shakirn laughed as if everything was a joke, Shelly slid the 007 pocket knife out of her bag. Sha reached over and grabbed a half smoked blunt from out of the ash tray oblivious to the potential danger lurking nearby.

Shelly flicked the knife open, and as Sha turned back to face her, Shelly was the one who now wore a wicked grin. It was such a wicked grin! Without warning she thrust the knife through the window and stabbed Sha in the face! He fell back, blood shooting like a fountain, but Shelly was in a blind rage. She stabbed him over and over again in the face, neck, and body, before finally leaving the knife protruding from his chest and running off into the night.

A medical examiner would later determine that Shakim had been stabbed twenty-seven times.

CHAPTER 43

Tasia and Steve strolled through the huge hotel lobby as if they were an official couple. There was mild traffic as people came and went; couples dressed in evening attire dined at one of the two restaurants on the premises, guests patronized the gift shop and rented cars from the Enterprise car rental agency in the lobby, and yet others were standing around just chilling.

Steve had his head held high with pride as he made his way toward the elevators with his arm draped around the baddest bitch in the vicinity. Steve's affection and behavior made Tasia a bit uncomfortable because it reminded her of compassion. The gentleness he used when he touched her communicated warmth, and made her feel protected. Yet, Tasia knew that Steve was the enemy! He didn't truly care about her.

He was just like all the others, interested in one thing. Pussy!

'He's being all sweet and acting like a gentleman just so he can get some Pussy' Tasia thought as they rode the elevator to the fifth floor.

"How many women do you seduce like this on a daily basis?" Tasia asked suddenly.

Steve looked at her intently, wondering where the question came from.

"Can I plead the fifth?" Steve countered, in reference to the fifth amendment of the United States Constitution that allows citizens the right to not incriminate themselves.

Tasia just rolled her eyes as the elevator delivered them to the fifth floor and Steve led the way down the hall to the room.

Once inside the room, Steve grabbed Tasia by both hands and he began walking backwards until he was sitting on the Queen size bed.

He lifted Tasia's tight black tee exposing her bare chest and began sucking on her stomach, using his tongue to play with her belly ring.

Tasia gasped as she assisted Steve by pulling her black tee over her head and tossing it to the floor. Steve had his hands under her mini skirt gripping her firm ass, spreading the cheeks apart before smoothly slipping two fingers into the sea of wetness at the end of the rainbow.

"Mmmmmmmm!" Tasia threw her head back and began playing with her breast while she grinded on Steve's fingers. Steve wasn't selfish at all, Tasia felt as if it was all about her.

'Damn,' Steve thought as he inserted another finger, 'this pussy is wetter than a mutha fucker!'

Tasia's breathing became irregular as Steve fucked her with his hand, and kissed and sucked all around her mid section. Tasia was bucking on his hand and Steve was so hard it felt as if his cock would burst from its skin!

"Get your ass out of that skirt!" He demanded as he stood up and began to undress.

Tasia did as she was told, stepping out of the skimpy skirt. She no longer wasted time wearing any underwear.

Steve grabbed her and threw his tongue in her mouth as he felt her up, gently massaging where ever he touched. Tasia was handling the standard seven with precision as she stroked the snake up and down with her delicate hands. Steve thought he was going to bust right there! He pushed Tasia back on the bed and immediately began sucking her breast, pinching the nipples and then sucking like a hungry infant.

Tasia was caught up in the rapture.

"Oooh, Steve!" she whimpered.

All of Tasia's previous lovers were either less experienced or their selfish asses were only concerned with their own nut. Steve on the other hand was making love to her.

Ole boy slowly made his way down to Tasia's garden. Just knowing where he was headed had Tasia going crazy! Steve played around, sucking on her inner thighs, licking and blowing softly until baby girl couldn't take it anymore. Tasia grabbed his head and pushed it to the main course! She was in her groove, winding on Steve's face.

"Right there, right there . . . ooh, that's my spot!" Tasia cried, and shortly after she was screaming that she was cumming!

Steve feasted on her juices, his face shining like patent leather. Tasia collapsed on the bed, her hands still gripping Steve's head.

"What the fuck are you doing to me?" she wanted to know.

Steve broke away from her hold, standing erect in two senses.

He looked down at Tasia's body and couldn't believe how perfect she was.

Tasia was watching him watching her, "Come on, Steve

. . . come and get this pussy," she pleaded seductively.

Steve climbed on the bed and mounted her, spreading her legs wide open before entering the depths of her being.

'Dammit man! This pussy is tight,' Steve thought as he looked into Tasia's eyes.

"Baby girl," Steve said as he delivered long strokes with a slow tempo, "Don't think I'm a sucker, but, no bull-shit . . . I think I'm in love with you."

Tasia was meeting his strokes, throwing the pussy at him.

"You don't even know me, Steve," she reminded him.

"I'm knowing you now . . . I know your beauty, God blessed you to make a man weak . . . it's not my fault that you're so beautiful. I'm weak because of the way that God created you, I'm telling you . . . I think I'm in love with you."

Steve's words penetrated Tasia's soul, and as she shared the good feeling of beautiful love making she understood how that feeling could make a person weak. Regardless of gender, race, or age, sex made people feel good.

Tasia closed her eyes so that she didn't have to look at Steve.

She was overtaken by guilt and the realization that Jeff wasn't' necessarily a bad person. He was only guilty of allowing himself to become weak. The same way Steve was weak now.

Tasia opened her eyes and Steve leaned down and licked her lips. He kissed her and put that standard seven on her properly. Tasia started crying!

"Is it good to you?" Steve asked as he kissed away her tears, "You make a nigga feel special, you know that, right? You make a nigga never wanna leave you . . . I can't believe you finally gave me some play."

Steve flipped her over a few times, twisted her up like a pretzel until he couldn't take it anymore and then he exploded inside of her. Afterward they laid there with him holding her closely, and Tasia cried some more. Steve thought Shorty was emotional from the mind blowing sex they just shared and he was mentally patting himself on the back as he soothed her with soft words. He snuggled against Tasia until he heard her snoring.

'Yes!' he thought, *'I fucked her pretty little ass to sleep. I'm a bad mutha fucker!'*

Steve eased out of the bed and quietly made his way to the bathroom so he could reward himself with a steaming hot shower.

It was Jeff's fifth time attending the HIV/AIDS support group, and at this particular meeting David Thomas had brought along a woman whom he introduced simply as Linda, and she had an incredible story to tell.

Linda had been raped at knife point by a man that pulled her into an alley in Midtown, a few blocks away from where she worked. When she learned that she was HIV Positive as a result of the rape, she began snorting heroin as a way to escape from what she described as a living nightmare.

"I started getting high again. I had been clean for over five years and then that happens . . . I didn't think I deserved what God was allowing me to go through. Before long I found myself on the streets with nowhere to go."

While Linda was homeless, she was raped two more

times by men that didn't believe her when she told them that she was HIV Positive.

Jeff was amazed by all of the stories that he heard, and he was happy that he had had the strength and courage to share his own story. Talking about it was therapeutic.

When Jeff made it back to four upper he was in good spirits, and even more so when he saw that he had mail.

'Oh shoot,' he thought as he looked at the return address on the letter, *'It's from Chip!'*

Jeff tore the envelope open immediately once he was in his cell. It was only one page, but, Jeff sat on his bed and read every word eagerly.

DEAR JEFF,

WHAT'S GOOD? I KNOW I'M PROBABLY THE LAST PERSON YOU EXPECTED TO HEAR FROM, BUT, IT'S ONLY RIGHT THAT I REACH OUT TO YOU. I'M SURE YOU HEARD WHAT HAPPENED WITH ME, AND THAT'S A GOOD THING AND A BAD THING. IT'S BAD BECAUSE I'M SITTING IN JAIL WITH NOT ONE, BUT TWO HOMOCIDES UNDER MY BELT. MY LAWYER THINKS I'LL BE LUCKY TO RECEIVE FIFTY TO LIFE. UNBELIEVABLE, RIGHT? YEAH I KNOW, BUT, IT'S ALL GOOD BECAUSE NOW I CAN TAKE RESPONSIBILITY FOR THE OTHER HOMOCIDE . . . THE ONE THAT YOU'RE LOCKED UP FOR. MY LAWYER SAID THEY FOUND MY BLOOD AT THE SCENE OF THE CRIME AND THAT THEY HAVE AT LEAST TWO PEOPLE WHO ARE SAYING THAT I WAS THE TRIGGER MAN. HOMIE, I DON'T KNOW WHERE THEY'RE GETTING THEIR INFORMATION FROM AND FRANKLY I DON'T CARE, THE BOTTOM LINE IS I KNOW

IT'S NOT FROM YOU! MY LAWYER ASSURED ME THAT YOU WERE NOT COOPERATING WITH THEM PEOPLE IN NO WAY, AND FOR THAT JEFF, I THANK YOU! YOU COULD'VE EASILY SACRAFICED MY ASS FOR YOURS BUT YOU DIDN'T. ANYWAY, THEY ALREADY DID A DNA TESTING, AND I SIGNED A NOTARIZED AFFADAVIT STATING THAT I WAS THE ONE THAT KILLED OLE BOY, SO, HOPEFULLY YOU'LL BE OUT OF HERE SOON. BUT, DO ME A FAVOR, JEFF . . . WHEN YOU GET OUT, HOLD ME DOWN. I WON'T NEED A LOT, BUT WHENEVER YOU CAN SEND A COUPLE OF DOLLARS I SURE WOULD APPRECIATE IT. I'M SORRY FOR ALL THAT I PUT YOU THROUGH AND I HOPE YOU'RE NOT UPSET WITH ME. KEEP YOUR HEAD UP AND BE EASY OUT THERE.

ONE,

CHIP MURDA!

Jeff jumped up from the bed!

"Yes!" he cried.

He read the letter again and again before jetting to call his lawyer. He had to wait for the phone, but, when he finally got through to Mr. Slotnick, the attorney was already aware of what was going on. In fact, Mr. Slotnick had good news.

"Jeff, they'll be calling you to court tomorrow. The district attorney, in light of the DNA and the signed affidavit, is asking that all charges against you be dismissed . . . "

Jeff dropped the phone and walked away! Chill and

another guy was off to the side waiting to use the phone and they seen what happened.

"You alright, son?" Chill asked with concern.

Tears were pouring down Jeff's face as he came back to the phone, "Yeah, Chill . . . they're throwing out my charges, man. I'm going home!"

Jeff picked up the phone and put it to his ear, "Mr. Slotnick? Yes, thank you for staying on the line . . . yes, okay, and I'll see you tomorrow . . . Yes, and thank you again, Mr. Slotnick . . . Bye!"

And Jeff hung up the phone. It was over. The worst part of it all was finally over, and Jeff could'nt help but to think about Tasia.

He wondered where she was at that moment.

Steve got out of the shower and dried off thoroughly before putting on the terry cloth robe.

He . . . *I* walked out of the bathroom and I couldn't believe my eyes! Tasia was sitting at the edge of the bed with my 9mm jammed into her mouth.

"Tasia, NO!" I yelled as I lunged toward the bed. The hollow click of the hammer landing on an empty chamber sent a wave of relief through my body.

"What the hell is wrong with you?" I asked as I tried to take the gun away from her.

"Get . . . off of me!" she screamed, fighting with me desperately, "Let me die! I don't ... deserve . . . to live!"

"Calm the fuck down! What do you mean you don't

deserve to live? you have a lot going for yourself, Tasia, you have every reason to live."

"Nooo! It's too late," Tasia cried as she abruptly stopped struggling with me. I pulled her to me and held her tightly. I kissed away her tears and rocked her back and forth in my futile attempt to bring peace within the realms of chaos.

"It's never too late to live, baby girl. Don't let nobody tell you no different, you hear me?" I whispered, but I was in for a wakeup call.

"You don't understand, Steve! I'm going to hell for what I did, but I'm sorry. I'm sooo sorry Steve, please forgive me."

I just sat there with a jackass look on my face, "I'm confused, Tasia. You're sorry for what? What are you sorry for?"

That's when baby girl dropped the bomb.

"I'm sick, Steve! I'm HIV Positive, and I've been running around having unprotected sex with people . . . now I probably gave it to you. All of this so I could get back at my boyfriend, he betrayed me--"

She may as well have been speaking a different language because from that point on I had no understanding. It was as if I was having an out of body experience. I watched as I picked up my 9mm and jacked a live round into the chamber.

Clack-clack!

That got Tasia's attention, and she looked at me as if she no longer wanted to die. But she was right, it was too late! I stood up with my finger on the trigger and aimed my gun at her pretty little face that was now filled with fear . . . and I squeezed!

I pulled the trigger over and over again until the gun locked back, an indication that the once full clip was now empty. Then I just stood there breathing hard for I don't know how long.

I was discombobulated.

The sound of the phone ringing brought me out of my zone!

'Damn, what the fuck I done now?' I thought as I looked around the room nervously. I tossed the empty gun on the bed and hurried to answer the phone.

"Yeah?" I asked, trying my best to sound normal.

"Is everything okay?" the person asked on the other end of the phone with a voice filled with concern.

"No, I mean yeah, why?" I asked stumbling over my words.

"The guest, they're reporting gunshots being fired in the hotel, the police are on the way."

"Nah, I didn't hear no shooting . . . it was probably on another floor," I said trying to buy some time.

"Are you sure everything is okay?"

Damn, I could hear in the dumb ass arab's voice that he didn't believe me.

"Eat a mutha fuckin' dick!" I yelled and slammed the phone down.

I began pacing around the room. My dick finally dragged my ass into the dirt. All the time I was thinking I was strong, I was the mutha fuckin' man, but all the while I was nothing more than a weak ass trick. I let my private parts control me! I just had to fuck everything that was moving, and now look! I was in a hotel room with a dead bitch lying in her own blood, and nine times out of ten I was infected with an ailment that didn't have a cure. HIV was unbiased! It killed people indiscriminately.

A loud knocking at the door damn near scared the shit out of me!

"Open up, it's the police!"

Oh shit! Damn, damn, damn! Before I could decide what to do, the door came crashing in!

"Get down on the floor! NOW!" Blue suits filled the room!

They handled me as if I was a sleeper cell down with Al-Qaeda!

I felt a foot on my head as an officer roughly put my hands behind my back and slapped the handcuffs on as tight as he could.

"You have the right to remain silent . . ."

They could've missed me with that bullshit because I wasn't listening. As I was dragged off to jail my mind was on one thing . . . how did my life take such a horrible turn in such a short period of time. Then all at once it came to me, I had a defense! Tasia said she was HIV Positive . . . she intentionally tried to kill me! No jury in America would find me guilty after hearing the facts. All I had to do was declare temporary insanity!

I was shuffled around for hours being processed. I went from bullpen to bullpen until I made it to a cell that was right next to the courtroom. That's when a lawyer came to see me. Mr. Schwartz. A big fat Jewish guy that I knew at once was a public defender. Being that it was an open and closed case I decided to use him. I explained that I could pay him handsomely to get me vindicated, then I told him exactly what happened. When we went in front of the judge I entered a plea of not guilty, and Mr. Schwartz requested that the autopsy performed on the deceased include an HIV test.

It was a week later and I was on Rikers Island when good ole Mr. Schwartz paid me a visit.

"I have some bad news for you young man," he said as I took a seat across from him.

"Bad news?" I repeated, wondering how my situation could possibly get any worse than it already was.

"Yes, bad news . . . very bad," Mr. Schwartz said in a monotone as he shuffled around a few papers, "The lab results came back, and . . . the report confirms that the deceased was actually HIV negative. That being the case, you no longer have a defense and I will not be able to represent you . . . I hope you understand."

No, I didn't understand! Nothing was making any sense! If Tasia was HIV negative then why did she want to kill herself? And why the hell did she tell me that she was HIV Positive?

Then it dawned on me, she must've really believed that she was HIV Positive. For some reason or another, she thought that she had been infected with the deadly disease and she knowingly tried to transmit it to as many people as possible. All Tasia had to do was get tested! If Tasia would've got tested . . . none of this would've never happened.

"DAMN!"

EPILOGUE

Immediately after his release, Jeff became an advocate in the fight to educate the people in the communities about HIV and AIDS. He started his own non-profit organization and dedicated his life to the struggle.

Raheem and his mother took Shakim's death hard. In their eyes he wasn't a bad kid, he just caught some tough breaks. Shakim's mother, Beverly, showed up for her son's funeral, and Raheem talked her into migrating with them to Jacksonville, Florida. Beverly has enjoyed sobriety ever since.

A month after Steve was arrested for killing Tasia, he went to medical services in C-74 and requested to take an HIV/AIDS test. Three days later he learned that HE WAS HIV Positive.

Note to reader:

-Be smart and don't get involved in high risk sexual activities!

-If you insist on gambling with your life, USE PROTECTION!

-If you haven't been tested for HIV or AIDS, GET TESTED!

Recent breakthroughs in the field of medicine are ready and available to assist those who choose to get help. KNOWLEDGE IS POWER! Make a conscious decision today to educate yourself and others about HIV and AIDS. It's not over until it's over.

Step Ya Game Up Publishing
EVEN FICTION NEEDS TO BE BELIEVABLE!

P.O. Box 25706 • Charlotte, NC 28227

Order Form

Name: _____

Address: _____

City: _____ State: _____ Zip: _____

Qty.	Title	Price	Total
_____	**Tropical Illusions**	$15.00	_____
_____	**24 Hours To Live** (Coming Soon)	$15.00	_____
_____	**Anybody Could Be Touched** (Coming Soon)	$15.00	_____
_____	**The Star In The Mirror** (Coming Soon)	$15.00	_____

Subtotal: _____

Shipping fees: _____

Total: _____

Books will be shipped within 7 business days once payment has been processed. All shipments will go out media mail. First book ($3.95); each additional book is $1.50 per book. No personal checks will be accepted. Make institutional checks or money orders payable to: **Step Ya Game Up Publishing** or go to **www.stepyagameuppublishing.com** to place an order.

STEP YA GAME UP PUBLISHING
EVEN FICTION NEEDS TO BE BELIEVABLE!

P.O. Box 25706 • Charlotte, NC 28227

Order Form

Name: _____

Address: _____

City: _____ **State:** _____ **Zip:** _____

Qty.	Title	Price	Total
_____	**Tropical Illusions**	$15.00	_____
_____	**24 Hours To Live** (Coming Soon)	$15.00	_____
_____	**Anybody Could Be Touched** (Coming Soon)	$15.00	_____
_____	**The Star In The Mirror** (Coming Soon)	$15.00	_____

Subtotal: _____

Shipping fees: _____

Total: _____

Books will be shipped within 7 business days once payment has been processed. All shipments will go out media mail. First book ($3.95); each additional book is $1.50 per book. No personal checks will be accepted. Make institutional checks or money orders payable to: **Step Ya Game Up Publishing** or go to **www.stepyagameuppublishing.com** to place an order.

STEP YA GAME UP PUBLISHING
EVEN FICTION NEEDS TO BE BELIEVABLE!

P.O. Box 25706 • Charlotte, NC 28227

Order Form

Name: _____

Address: _____

City: _____ **State:** _____ **Zip:** _____

Qty.	Title	Price	Total
____	**Tropical Illusions**	$15.00	_____
____	**24 Hours To Live** (Coming Soon)	$15.00	_____
____	**Anybody Could Be Touched** (Coming Soon)	$15.00	_____
____	**The Star In The Mirror** (Coming Soon)	$15.00	_____

Subtotal: _____

Shipping fees: _____

Total: _____

Books will be shipped within 7 business days once payment has been processed. All shipments will go out media mail. First book ($3.95); each additional book is $1.50 per book. No personal checks will be accepted. Make institutional checks or money orders payable to: **Step Ya Game Up Publishing** or go to **www.stepyagameuppublishing.com** to place an order.

STEP YA GAME UP PUBLISHING
EVEN FICTION NEEDS TO BE BELIEVABLE!

P.O. Box 25706 • Charlotte, NC 28227

Order Form

Name: _____

Address: _____

City: _____ State: _____Zip: _____

Qty.	Title	Price	Total
_____	**Tropical Illusions**	$15.00	_____
_____	**24 Hours To Live** (Coming Soon)	$15.00	_____
_____	**Anybody Could Be Touched** (Coming Soon)	$15.00	_____
_____	**The Star In The Mirror** (Coming Soon)	$15.00	_____

Subtotal: _____

Shipping fees: _____

Total: _____

Books will be shipped within 7 business days once payment has been processed. All shipments will go out media mail. First book ($3.95); each additional book is $1.50 per book. No personal checks will be accepted. Make institutional checks or money orders payable to: **Step Ya Game Up Publishing** or go to **www.stepyagameuppublishing.com** to place an order.